Mehdi Charef was born in Algeria in 1952. He came to live in Paris in 1964 when his father could afford to bring the family to France. On leaving school, he worked in an engineering factory in the Paris suburbs until the publication of *Tea In The Harem* in 1983. Following the novel's success, he was asked by Costa-Gavras to direct a film of the book. This won the Prix Jean Vigo for the best first film at the Cannes Festival.

Critical acclaim for *Tea In The Harem*

'Grabbed me from page one and never let go' Hanif Kureishi

'Scorches the emotions like the very best Chester Himes' *Le Nouvel Observateur*

'. . . possesses writing that is both dazzling and economical and a moral and aesthetic elegance that does not judge. The greatest attribute of this extraordinary first novel is its thirst for life' *Le Quotidien de Paris*

'The tea Mehdi Charef serves up is not "by appointment to H.M. The Queen". Rather it is a heady brew, part despair, part revenge and part sludge' *Nouvelles Littéraires*

'*Tea In The Harem* does not wallow in the world it depicts, it expresses the urge to "get out". It is a dry, fast and ferocious book' *Figaro Magazine*

'By the time you have forgotten the novels you read over the summer, you will remember the truth, the despair, the poignant gaucheness of *Tea In The Harem* . . . It is the true voice of those who never speak' *L'Express*

'He describes everyday hurts and bruises as if they were distinctive characteristics of the human condition. This unadorned voice goes straight to the heart. Listen to it!' *Le Monde*

TEA
· IN THE ·
HAREM

Mehdi Charef

Translated by
Ed Emery

A complete catalogue record for this book can
be obtained from the British Library on request

The right of Mehdi Charef to be identified as the author
of this work has been asserted by him in accordance
with the Copyright, Designs and Patents Act 1988

First published as *Le thé au harem d'Archi Ahmed* by
Mercure de France, Paris 1983

First published in 1989 by Serpent's Tail,
4 Blackstock Mews, London N4 2BT

website: www.serpentstail.com

Printed in Great Britain by Mackays of Chatham, plc

10 9 8 7 6 5 4 3

for my mother Mebarka,
who can't read.

TEA
· IN THE ·
HAREM

Majid is down on his knees tinkering with his bike. He wipes the grease off his hands with a rag. His bike is an ageing Norton that is beginning to wheeze at the first sign of difficulty. When he comes to a hill these days, he virtually has to get off and push it, and the other evening he was choked to find himself being overtaken by a truck on the motorway to Pontoise. Basically, the bike's past it. Repairing it is going to take money, and money is one thing that Majid doesn't have. He reaches over the inspection lamp and takes a long, hard look at the engine. The propect of being stuck without transport annoys him. Finally he admits defeat, puts the bike away, unplugs the lamp and comes up out of the basement, padlocking the door as he goes. Out in the damp, gloomy corridor, with its acrid smell of piss and shit, he lights a cigarette and makes for the exit.

When he reaches the steps leading up to the ground-floor entrance he changes his mind. Halfway up he does an about-turn and retraces his steps. He walks to the last alcove at the far end of the basement. He pauses and stares into the darkness.

The dark, poky cellar is occupied by a mattress, whose springs have split the material just where it's

stained with piss, and a broken fridge with its door
hanging open, presumably dumped there by someone at dead of night. In among the junk, surrounded
by a strong hospital smell, lies little Farid. He's
nineteen years of age and looks fifteen; his face is
dry and drawn, under an adolescent beard, and he's
completely out of it.

Farid is lying on a makeshift bed of Outspan
orange boxes, with an old suitcase as his pillow
– brown mock-leather, with its corners all dented.
Majid walks quietly up to the lad and looks at
him. Farid doesn't even notice him. In his right
hand he's holding a dirty rag, which is impreg-
nated with ether. Every now and then he raises
it, slowly and with difficulty, to take a sniff. 'Hi,
Rusty!' says Majid, barely raising his voice. He gets
no reply, so he leans over and whispers to him a
second time.

Rusty moves his head a bit and looks at Majid
through half-closed eyes. His face is a blank. His
eyes have a distant look. His pathetic, sickly smile
reveals a row of yellow teeth. In a vague gesture,
he reaches out his left hand to shake hands with
his visitor. Then he takes another long sniff at his
disgusting rag.

Majid watches him for a moment, at a loss for
what to say. Farid weighs barely forty kilos, and
is obviously dying – but who gives a shit? Everybody on the estate knows that he's a glue-sniffer.
They say he's sniffed everything there is to sniff,
and drugged himself on everything there is to get
drugged on, including petrol. There was a period
when he was getting high on Rustine puncture-kit

rubber solution, and that's where he'd got his nick-name, 'Rusty'.

Majid didn't find it funny, but his friend Pat thought it was hysterical. 'Rusty. . .!'

Majid pulls out a cigarette and lays it next to the little bottle of ether on Rusty's empty belly. Rusty lies there, not moving, his hand cupped over his nose. Then he tips a couple of drops of ether onto the rag in the palm of his skeletal hand and takes another sniff. Majid begins to get impatient. Dusty cobwebs hang from the ceiling of the cellar that Farid has made his home, and the ceiling is oozing damp. The walls are covered with slogans, graffiti and crude drawings. In the dark you can just make out half-words and phrases in red chalk: 'fuck', 'piss off', 'I wouldn't mind. . .', that sort of thing.

Majid tries to fathom the meaning of it all. But there's nothing to understand.

'What a shit-heap,' he tells himself. 'Best thing'd be to get the fuck out. . .'

He has his whole life spread out before him, but all he feels is a sense of despair, a creepy feeling which tingles in the small of his back and sends a chill down his spine. The best thing for him would be to get his cowboy boots on and not hang about asking questions.

Majid leaves Rusty, cigarette in hand, and returns to the entrance-hall, with its strong, white neon light. It feels better here. More space. He runs into Mr Levesque from the flat across the landing. He's waiting for the lift. Majid greets him, and Levesque responds with a grudging smile and a glazed look. He's got a gutful of Ricard, and he's on his way home, drunk as usual, after an evening at the bar. Majid can't remember a day when he's seen him sober, or even halfway coherent. The lift arrives and each of them steps back to make way for the other. The smell of pastis in the lift is vile; Majid finds his neighbour's breath hard to stomach.

Levesque swears when he realizes he's trodden in a pool of piss. Majid turns away, looks at the floor, and says:

'Must have been the kids. . . or a dog. . .'

Levesque, his bloated face reddened by alcohol and by the effect of the cold outside, says nothing. As far as he's concerned, it's the Arabs who piss in the lift and bring down the tone of the building. That's why Majid feels obliged to offer his explanation. Arabs don't have dogs. Not usually, anyway.

Poor bloody dogs – locked in the flats all day long waiting for their masters to come home from work to take them out. No sooner are they in the lift than their bladders give out and they piss on the floor. And dogs' piss stinks. The delights of inner-city life.

They get out of the lift at the third floor. Majid goes straight into his flat without knocking. The front door's always open.

Levesque, on the other hand, has to ring his doorbell several times before his wife comes to let him in. He has a job getting through the door.

Majid takes off his shoes and heads straight down the corridor to his room. His is a large family, and his brothers and sisters are round the front-room table arguing over their homework. His mother – Malika – is a solidly-built Algerian woman. As she stands in the kitchen, she sees her son sneaking down the corridor.

'Majid!'

Without turning round he goes straight into his room. 'Yeah?'

'Go and get your father.'

'In a minute!'

Malika bangs her pan down on the draining-board and shouts:

'Straight away!'

He puts the Sex Pistols on the record player and plays *God Save the Queen* at full blast. Punk rock. That way he doesn't have to listen to his mother. He lies back on the bed, hands behind his head, and shuts his eyes to listen to the music. But his mum isn't giving up so easily:

'Did you hear what I said?'

She speaks lousy French, with a weird accent, and gesticulates like an Italian. Majid raises his eyes to the ceiling, with the air of a man just returned from a hard day's work, and in a voice of tired irritation he replies:

'Lay off, ma, I'm whacked!'

Since she only half understands what he's saying, she goes off the deep end. She loses her temper, and her African origins get the upper hand. She starts ranting at him in Arabic.

She comes up to the end of the bed and shakes him, but he doesn't budge. She dries her hands on the apron which is forever about her waist, switches off the stereo, tucks back the tuft of greying hair that hangs across her forehead, and begins abusing her son with all the French insults she can muster – 'Layabout. . . Hooligan. . . Oaf. . .' and suchlike, all in her weird pronunciation. Majid pretends he doesn't understand. He answers coolly, just to irritate her:

'What'd you say? I didn't understand a word.'

By now his mother is beside herself. 'Didn't understand, didn't understand. . . Oh, God. . .!' and she slaps her thighs.

She tries to grab him by the ear, but he ducks out of range. Finally he admits defeat and gets off the bed, scratching his head.

His mother follows him:

'Yes. Layabout! Hooligan!'

While she continues ranting at him and calling him every name under the sun, he puts the Sex Pistols back in their sleeve and gives a long-suffering sigh.

Then Malika informs her son, in Arabic, that she's going to see the Algerian consul. 'They'll come and get you, and you'll have to do your military service. *That* way you'll learn about your country. . . *and* you'll learn the language. . . *that'll* make a man of you. You say you won't do your military service like all your friends have to, but if you don't you'll never get your papers, and me neither. You'll lose your citizenship, and you'll never be able to go to Algeria because you'll end up in prison. *That's* where you'll end up. No country, no roots, no nothing. You'll be finished.'

Majid understands the occasional phrase here and there, and his reply is subdued, because whatever he says is bound to hurt her.

'I never asked to come here. If you hadn't decided to come to France, I wouldn't be "finished", would I, eh? So leave me alone, will you?'

She continues haranguing him, unleashing all the bitterness that is locked in her heart. It's not unusual for her to end up crying.

Someone knocks at the front door.

'Who is it?' she shouts, still furious.

She leaves the room and Majid flops down on the bed, reflecting that for a long time he's been neither French nor Arab. He's the son of immigrants – caught between two cultures, two histories, two languages, and two colours of skin. He's neither black nor white. He has to invent his own roots, create his own reference points. For the moment, he's waiting. . . waiting. . . He doesn't want to have to think about it. . .

'Malika. . . come, come. . . dad's hitting mummy.'

Fabienne Levesque makes way for Malika to go

on ahead. Malika bursts into the next-door flat like a ten-ton truck, calling on her god as she goes:

'Ah! Allah! Ah! My God!'

You can hear Mrs Levesque's screams from the landing. Majid presses the reject button on the stereo and goes off into the front room.

The flat's deserted. The whole family's gone off with their mother to watch the action chez Levesque.

Majid switches on the TV and sits on a rickety chair; he's hoping to steer clear of the Levesques tonight. The 'circus', as he puts it.

He knows the scenario. It often happens that old man Levesque tires of beating his wife with his fists and picks up a belt or a chair instead. Then Malika has to send Fabienne, or seven-year-old Eric, to fetch Majid. The kids arrive, terrified, shouting:

'Dad's got a knife!'

At this point Majid usually shifts himself. He carves a path through the screaming kids and the furniture, and sets about trying to calm Levesque – Bebert to his drinking pals – without having to use force on him.

Little Fabienne raises her trembling hands to her cheeks and screams:

'Mummy. . . mummy. . .'

The young boy, who has a bit of his father in him, is shouting:

'Stop it, dad, stop it!'

Malika tries to reason with Levesque. He's paralytic drunk and his eyes are red and full of hatred and violence. When Majid tries to intervene, he abuses him.

'Fuck off home, you black bastard. I'm going to see to this bitch!'

Malika ignores Levesque's insults, and hangs onto him. She only lets go when he begins to run out of steam. 'I'll kill the bitch!'

The 'bitch' is his wife Elise. She's got a bloody nose, because the first blow usually catches her unawares. Then she has to dodge round the table, trying to duck as best she can. When Levesque's in good form, he gets bored with chasing his wife and not getting his hands on her, and he tips the table over, together with everything that's on it. At this point things are getting serious, and help has to arrive pretty fast, because soon he'll corner his wife and start punching her in the face. Then she has to stay indoors for the best part of a fortnight, waiting for the bruising to disappear.

Even the kids take the most terrible beatings. And sometimes, blinded by the alcohol, he just lashes out at anyone in reach. A regular spectacle, which is his sole means of relating to his next-door neighbours. In the outside world they barely even acknowledge each other. That's the way it goes.

Finally, he begins to tire. When he's worn himself out shouting and threatening – all time held by mamma Malika, who is completely fearless – they take him to his room. They dump him on his bed and wait till he calms down, stops swearing, and begins to nod off. Sometimes he vomits, and his eyes become moist with tears that have no obvious rhyme or reason. The swearing becomes an indistinct mumbling, and he falls asleep. Out like a light, with his head hanging over the side of the bed where he's been sick. Her night's work done, Malika takes her kids home, leaving Elise – a woman of thirty-six who looks much older – standing at her front door with a scary night ahead of her. She's got fear in her guts, her hair's all over the place, and her face is marked by bruising and the traces of tears. In a voice that is weary, awkward and full of shame, she says:

'Thanks ever so much, Malika, thanks. . .'

Malika doesn't reply. She tucks her hair back under her scarf and begins to scold the kids as they hang round her apron-strings squabbling. She tells them to behave themselves, otherwise she'll do the same as 'm'sieu Livisque'.

'Understand?' she says, and raises a warning finger.

Majid's still in the front room staring at the TV when his mum returns. There are no armchairs in the room, no plants, nothing at all by way of decoration. Just a bed against the wall, covered with a dark green drape, on which the kids scramble for the best position to watch TV.

There are four rooms in the flat. Little Mehdi sleeps on the bed in the front room. Majid shares a room with his father. Malika sleeps with the eldest girl, Amaria, who's doing so well at school that Malika's bought her a typewriter on credit, instead of leasing one like before. Ounissa, at seven years old, is the youngest and Majid, at eighteen, is the eldest. All the children except Majid were born in France. The parents had married young, and then they emigrated. They wanted to send their kids to school so that they could grow up to be doctors. . . lawyers. . . schoolteachers. . . the Third World dream.

But already Majid and his father are unemployed. . . 'Go get your father!' Malika repeats. Majid doesn't move from his chair. To show his mother that he's ignoring her, he starts pulling faces at his kid sister. His mother explodes and starts yelling again in Arabic:

'I suppose you expect *me* to go out looking for your father, eh?'

He pulls another face.

And his mother continues, in French:

'I'm tired. I'm sick. I work in the morning, doing the cleaning at the school, and you just stay in bed. I do the cleaning at the office in the evening, and then I have to do the housework. I'm tired, me, tired. And you. . . layabout. . .! It's me who has to go to the town hall, to the welfare, to the social security. . . My legs ache. . . And you, out gadding about all day. . . Oh, my God. . .'

Meanwhile the kids are playing or getting on with their homework. They're used to their mother complaining about her fate. She goes back to the kitchen to stir the rice, and then returns to insult her son again. This time he cracks, and goes to put on his shoes. Amaria lays the table, and the kids put away their homework, still keeping one eye on the TV. Majid heads down the corridor, and as he leaves the flat he hears his mother saying:

'Aren't you ashamed of yourself, sponging off your poor mother?'

As he comes out of the lift into the hallway, Majid finds old man Pelletier standing there, a solidly-built fifty-year-old, who is extremely proud of his dog – a large and evil-looking Alsatian that he's got on a leash. The animal lifts its head and Majid has to step out of its way. This makes Pelletier happy. He smiles. This estate runs on fear. It's the local currency of exchange, since people have so little else to give. It seems easier to create a climate of fear by staying shut up indoors with an Alsatian at your feet, rather than going out and facing up to people in an attempt to understand them and understand yourself.

Fear dominates this estate and its inhabitants. There's an atmosphere of dread, or so it seems, with all these young people taking drugs, thieving, raping old women and so on. It's madness. People are talking about getting guns to defend themselves. The security firms and locksmiths are making a killing, what with the demand for new locks, and for anti-theft alarms that ring and screech and squirt liquids and explode. . . take your pick, there's a new leaflet comes through your letterbox every day.

They even say that women get raped in the basements of the flats.

But when you've got a big Alsatian you feel less afraid. . . You can walk up to a group of young people hanging out at the entrance to a tower block; you can walk right up to them and provoke them a bit. You could almost go looking for trouble, with a monster of an animal like that, its snout in a muzzle, waiting for just one thing: the order to attack. The muzzle seems to make these fearsome animals even meaner.

As for the dog's owner, he's walking tall. He struts about like he owns the place. He's not scared of these young thugs, these wankers, these burners of cars. . .

Majid is careful not to turn his back on Pelletier and the dog. He doesn't trust them. Turn your back and the dog might just go for you. They glare at each other. They know each other. One time they almost came to blows over Pelletier's daughter, the one who drives all the young men on the estate crazy with her pretty little arse tucked into her tight blue jeans. Majid fancied her, and she fancied him, but old man Pelletier keeps a watchful eye on her boyfriends. An Arab boyfriend? No chance!

As he crosses the street, Majid zips up his jacket. The evening is cool, almost cold. He lights a cigarette and crosses from Azalea Drive, where he lives, to Acacia Drive. All the streets on the estate are named after flowers. Flower City – that's what they call it!

Acres of concrete. The smell of piss. Cars, cars and more cars. And dog turds. Row after row of

tall, soulless apartment blocks. No joy, no laughter, just heartache and pain. A huge estate, sand-
wiched between motorways, ringed by factories and
by police. The estate's got a tiny playground for the
kids, but it's been boarded up.

Flower City!

Concrete walls, covered with slogans. . . Cries
from the heart. . . anti-racist graffiti in the form of
raised fists. . . great long cocks and hairy testicles
spray-painted down the walls.

Boys' names and girls' names, over hearts pierced
by Cupid's arrow. Or things like: 'Annie F. is on
the pill', probably written by the family opposite,
to get their own back. Anything to make someone
else's miserable life more miserable still. Spray it
on the walls. That way you feel yourself superior,
even though you're in the same shit as everyone
else. Or things like, 'Fatima B. had an abortion' –
the sort of thing guaranteed to cause a riot in the
girl's family, with the inevitable bawling-out. . .
and then the beating. . . and then maybe blood. . .
and then the police. If a girl happens to feel ill,
she'd best not go to the doctor on the estate, or
to the local hospital, because everyone will assume
she needs an abortion. People will grass you up for
anything – for getting drunk. . . for screwing. . . for
smoking a joint.

Everyone spying on each other, and everyone
pretending that it isn't really happening. There's
no such thing as privacy in these flats. When it
comes to hitting back at your neighbours, anything
goes, and they're more than happy to wash other
people's dirty linen in public.

Majid cuts across the car park to Acacia Drive. It's half past eight. Time for the evening's comedy show on TV, or the feature film on the other channel. No more Alsatians crapping on the grass verges – they've all gone back indoors with their masters, who parade their dogs round the estate as if they were loaded guns, with a sadistic smile on their faces that says, 'Feel free to come and burgle my place while I'm out at work. Just remember – you won't get out alive!'

Every time Majid meets an Alsatian and its owner on the estate, he spits. Both parties glare at each other and carry on walking. It would take almost nothing – the tiniest spark – to cause an explosion.

As Pat says, one day it's going to be war between the parents and the young people on the estate. A war to the death. When he gets to Acacia House, Majid heads for the hallway.

Here he finds his pals. There's Bengston the West Indian; Thierry, aka Clicker; James, born in France of Algerian parents; Jean-Marc, thrown out by his dad and now sleeping rough in a basement of one of the flats; Bibiche, another first-generation Franco-Algerian, nicknamed 'Chopin' because when he was young he dreamed of being a pianist (these days he no longer dreams – he's settled for a guitar); and Anita, the only girl in the gang, who's always there in the thick of things. Left school; no job; the daughter of an Algerian father and a French mother. Her dad went back to Algeria one day and that was the last they heard of him. And then there's Pat – 'our Pat', as he's known. Big-boned, with the build of a furniture-removal man and not too bright. A swagger in his walk and a nervous habit of brushing his blond hair back out of his eyes. A grade-one bigmouth, and always bottom of the class.

Majid shakes the hand of anyone he's not seen during the day. Some of them are sitting on the steps of the entrance hall; others are lounging against parked cars.

Majid shakes hands with Bengston, who's in the mood to take the piss:

'Looking for daddy, are we?'

Majid gives him a threatening look:

'Up yours!'

'Yours too,' comes the reply.

Bibiche stops picking at his guitar, removes the match he's chewing, and says:

'Can't you stop that bloody racket. . .? I can't hear myself think.'

Thierry: 'Can't we even have a little chat, because Sir won't allow it?!'

Bibiche: 'You're just a load of wankers. What do you know about music, anyway?'

He stops playing his guitar and hits the button of his portable cassette player. Rock music blasts out.

Majid doesn't like people talking about his dad. It's guaranteed to put him in a bad mood. His pals know it, but they can't resist having a dig every now and then, just to wind him up. Majid doesn't find it funny. Anita decides to change the subject. She's shivering. She wraps her arms round herself and says:

'Not what you'd call warm, is it!'

She hunches her shoulders and her little weasel

face looks out from under the mass of long, black hair that keeps her neck warm. She smiles at Majid when he comes and sits next to her. When she half opens those moist, strawberry-coloured lips, you can see her fine, white teeth, and you long to caress them with your tongue. Her cheeks have the colour of a Maghreb sand dune in the rays of the setting sun. As for getting her into bed, though – no chance! Pigs would fly first! She's waiting for her Prince Charming – he'd have to be street-wise, into pinball and rock music, and he'd have to prefer buses to motorbikes, and be a bit of a dreamer. He'd pop out from between two brightly-painted tower blocks and whisk her away from this concrete jungle. She's so keen on this dream man that she's forever talking about him, and all the lads in the gang are ashamed of not being him. Because they sense, they know, that she would be utterly devoted to her dream man; she'd love him like crazy, to make up for lost time. And though we might not notice it, women have their ways of making up for lost time.

James's voice comes grumbling out of the corner where he's sitting apart from the others:

'That's fucking true, that is – where're we going to go this winter, now they've shut the club?'

'Hardly surprising that they shut it,' says Thierry, 'when certain people were turning up waving joints around.'

'"Certain people", what d'you mean "certain people"?' asks Bengston, sensing that he's being talked about. 'And I suppose you've never smoked a joint. . .?'

Thierry defends himself. 'I didn't mean that. I'm

just saying that if certain people had been a bit more careful, they wouldn't have shut the place.'

Pat crushes his dogend with the heel of his boot and chimes in:

'Anyway, what the fuck's it got to do with them if people want to smoke a bit of dope? All we want is a place where we can get together. What happens then is none of their business!'

'Anyway,' says Bengston, 'all these youth club leaders are just cops in disguise. So long as you just go to the club to play ping-pong, they leave you alone. But the minute you suggest doing something different they turn nasty and say it's not part of their "programme". Well, let me tell you, their "programme" comes straight from the cop-shop.'

He thumps his chest and stretches back the corners of his mouth in a characteristic grimace that shows he's annoyed:

'They set up clubs like this so's they can keep an eye on us, so as to keep us stuck in front of the telly instead of out there doing things. And nobody says anything – everyone's fed up, but nobody says a word.'

Thierry warms to the theme:

'If I meet that ponce of a social worker, I'll kick his fucking head in. He's the one who got the club closed. For fuck-all. Just because he found a joint on the premises. All he's good for is showing stupid cartoon films. Arsehole!'

'I like cartoon films,' Pat protests.

'Who asked you?' Thierry counters, angrily.

Pat advances on Thierry. 'How would you like your face pushed in, creep?'

Thierry holds his head high and fronts him out.

'Shut your mouth, shithead!'

Bibiche puts another tape in his cassette player and sighs irritatedly:

'Why don't you *all* shut up, so's we can hear the music?'

Thierry and Pat back off, still glaring at each other. Bengston observes mournfully:

'All set for a nice punch-up, and Chopin goes and blows it.

He looks at Chopin, pulls a face, and says:

'Eh, my old mate?'

Bengston gets up, dusts off the seat of his jeans and starts singing: 'We are bored, we are bored, we are bored. . .'

Bibiche has the cassette recorder to his ear: 'Why don't you go take a walk and stop bugging us?'

At this moment a man from one of the ground-floor flats opens a window next to where the gang are sitting and asks them, politely, almost regretfully:

'Could you be a bit quieter, lads, or go and talk somewhere else, because I've got kids sleeping in here.'

All you can see is the bloke's head behind the window. The young people ignore him, just staring at him vacuously, to hide a moment of embarrassment. Then Bengston laughs out loud and slaps his thighs; the others start laughing too. The tenant's bald head disappears. The window closes again.

Thierry gives the man two fingers.

Chopin can't resist passing comment:

'See what happens. . .? You and your big mouths!'

Quick as a flash, Bengston cuts in:

'Aren't we even allowed to talk in this fucking dump? Eh?'

He advances on Bibiche, gesticulating like a cartoon Italian:

'Me, I do what I want and I say what I want.'

As he reaches Bibiche, he grabs his cassette player and runs off to hide behind a parked car. Bibiche leaps up and rushes after him, chasing him round the cars.

Bibiche shouts and threatens him, but Bengston just rushes about laughing. He turns the music up full blast and starts dancing.

'Give it back here, you black bastard,' shouts Chopin. 'You don't know how to use it – you'll break it.'

The others laugh. Anita gets up.

'OK. See you. I've got to go.'

She heads off towards her tower-block, with her hands in the back pockets of her jeans.

Bibiche gives up and sits on the steps again, shaking his fist at Bengston.

'You dirty black. . .'

The 'dirty black. . .' is dancing around in the middle of the street, taunting Bibiche, and Bibiche mutters to Pat, who's sitting next to him:

'What do you do with an arsehole like that?!'

Bengston stops dancing about and shouts over to his pals:

'Right. I'm going to sing something. And I'm going to record it. OK?'

He takes the cassette player and starts fiddling with the controls. Bibiche threatens him:

'You break that and I'll do you!'

'Don't worry. I've got one of these too!' says Bengston.

It's getting late. Cold too. Time to put a jacket on. The lights are going out in people's windows. Silence descends on the estate. 'Ha!' he says. 'I know what I'll record. . . ha, ha!'

He grits his teeth and swells his stomach out. Then he presses on it.

'Be patient. It's coming.' His face contorts as he says: 'Don't move.'

The others stay put.

Majid laughs. Pat too. Thierry shakes his head in mock despair. Then Bengston gets his act under way. He grits his strong, white teeth – the teeth of a West Indian – and presses on his stomach again. He stands there, eyes closed, a picture of concentration. He puts the cassette player behind him, makes one final effort, and farts an enormous fart. Then he falls about, laughing and slapping his thighs.

The others fall about laughing too, all except for Bibiche, who gets up and goes to try to retrieve his cassette player, shouting: 'Lucky it doesn't record the smell, otherwise we'd all be dead.'

General hysterics again. Bengston is pleased – he's got the limelight and plays it for all it's worth. He bawls at the surrounding concrete: 'Right. Now we're going to listen to that magnificent fart again. Roll up, roll up! Ladies and Gentlemen! For the fart that sounds but doesn't smell! Your attention please!' The showman works his audience.

The estate is deathly quiet. He presses the button on the cassette player, but nothing happens. Not a peep. Thierry shouts, 'Try turning it up full.'

'I have,' the West Indian replies.

And just at that moment, the recorder lets out an enormous fart. They all double up in hysterics. Even Bibiche can't resist laughing.

'What an arsehole! There's only one black man like this in the whole of Paris, and *we* have to get stuck with him! Why us, for fuck's sake!'

Bengston leaves the tape running and does a little war-dance in the middle of the road. He gyrates slowly, holding the cassette player over his head like a trophy.

He closes his eyes and he sings.

Jean-Marc and Thierry clap hands in time with his singing. They improvise a little party. Bibiche has calmed down by now, and he picks up his guitar and joins in. Then, all of a sudden, crash! A bottle comes hurtling down and smashes into a thousand pieces a couple of yards from where Bengston is standing. Pandemonium! Bengston freezes for a moment, as he gathers his thoughts. He glances quickly at the window above, and dives for cover under the porch with the rest of the gang. Nobody says a word. They look at each other. Bengston is breathing hoarsely, as if he has silicosis. It's scared the pants off him. He graciously hands the cassette player back to Chopin, who says:

'You had a near miss, there, pal. You can thank the luck of a black man!'

He takes his head in his hands, as if relieved but still in a state of shock.

'Fuckin' hell – another few feet and it'd have killed me!'

Bengston is still shaking as he looks at the shattered glass in the road. 'Who do you reckon it was?' asks Thierry.

Bengston looks at him, wide-eyed.

'No idea. I looked up, but I didn't see anyone.'

Majid chips in:

'I suppose you expected advance warning. . .!'

'It's like that rifle shot a couple of months ago,' says Pat. 'The only reason they miss is because they're too scared to aim properly.'

'Bastards,' Bengston mutters to himself.

Bibiche comes out from under the porch and walks backwards down the steps, keeping a watchful eye on the upper storeys in case another bottle comes flying.

'Be careful,' Pat warns him. 'You'll probably find he's got a crateful up there. . .'

Bibiche takes a close look at the shattered fragments in the road, particularly the neck of the bottle.

Thierry asks:"

'What is it, Postillon or Gévéor?'

Bibiche doesn't answer. He's trying to get the label off the bottle.

Pat's in a comical mood:

'Doesn't look like Ricard this time round! Ha, ha.'

'This time of night it's more likely to be a brandy,' says Majid.

Chopin comes back under the porch, having finally detached the label. He holds it up to the light to read.

'Pastelvin.'

'What?' asks Bengston.

'Look – can't you read? It's written there – Pastelvin.'

They give each other blank looks.

'Pastelvin — that's top-class vino,' says Thierry, and he laughs.

'We'll just have to check the block out, floor by floor,' says Bengston.

'One thing we know — it didn't come from the ground floor or the first floor, OK?' says Thierry.

At this moment, Jean-Marc, who never says a lot at the best of times, decides to say something. He takes a long drag on the freshly-rolled joint and announces:

'Don't bother looking. It was my old man.'

They all turn and look at him. Titi frowns with surprise and looks at Pat. Jean-Marc blows out the smoke and closes his eyes.

'You sure what you're saying?' asks Titi. 'You really reckon it was your old man?'

Jean-Marc hands the joint to Bibiche:

'That's what I said. He gets the stuff from my grandad, out in the country.'

Bengston swears and pulls a box of matches out of his pocket:

'Well you can tell your beloved father that he's a bastard.'

'Don't worry. I already have. He threw me out.'

Bengston juggles with his box of matches and announces:

'I'm going to torch your old man's motor. It'll be a pile of ashes when he comes down in the morning.'

'That's not a bad idea, what you're saying there,' says Pat, approvingly. 'I'll come with you. We'll sort the bastard out.'

I don't know where he parks it. We'll find it, though,' says Thierry.

Bibiche gives the joint back to Jean-Marc and says slily:

'I bet you really love your dad, don't you!'

Jean-Marc doesn't respond. He takes the joint delicately in his fingers and raises it to his lips.

'OK. I'm off. . . got to go. . .' says Chopin.

'Don't worry – nobody's seen you with us,' Bengston replies, mockingly.

'Fuck off,' Chopin snorts as he pushes the hall door open.

His friends know that he'll exit from the other side of the tower block by cutting through the basement. That way, nobody sees where he's come from.

Somehow the night seems darker here than in other parts of town, as if it feels at home. The estate dies, and the footsteps of passers-by sound like echoing drum-beats. It feels like being stuck behind a wall in a cemetery in a strange village in the middle of nowhere, trying to find your way home.

The lads go off looking for the car that they're planning to burn. They go from one car park to the next, just like when they take a short-cut via the cemetery, kicking over flowers and gravestones as they go, only this time it's wing mirrors, car bumpers and windscreen wipers that get the treatment. Majid follows them for a moment, but then

changes his mind because he's remembered something.

'I've got to go look for my dad.'

The others pay no attention. They're thinking
about revenge. Majid walks off, then stops and
looks back. Pat calls after him:

'I'll see you later!'

'OK.'

He heads off down the street in the opposite direction, his hands buried in his jacket pockets. He turns the collar up. He walks like an animal looking for a way out of its cage. His baggy trousers flap in the wind as he walks. He has the air of a whole gang of hoodlums all rolled into one. The click-clack of his steel-tipped boots echoes across the bare, silent concrete.

He moves through the backstreets, weaving his way through the cars parked on the pavement. He finally emerges from the estate and walks down the main street. Here, on a corner, is the Arab café known as Chez Hamid.

This is the place where the town's immigrants – the bachelor workers, as they're known – come to drown their homesickness in a beer. Majid shakes hands with a few people and goes and stands at the bar. There's the sound of dominoes rattling on the tables, as the players call out their scores in poor French.

The air is heavy with a thick pall of smoke, which rises to the ceiling like a dancing shadow. The place is dimly-lit and noisy. Majid shakes hands with the barman, whom he knows, and turns to look at the little old man standing next to him. The man takes a drag on a cigarette that he's holding between two long, thin fingers that are stained with nicotine. His cheeks are hollow and ill-shaven. His black eyes peer out from under a pair of bushy eyebrows as he gazes into the mirror hanging on the other side of the bar. His elbows are resting on the damp counter. He doesn't budge. Majid pours his beer, taking care that it doesn't froth over the top of the glass. At the other end of the bar, the house prostitute, a big brunette with garish lipstick, is being picked up by a drunken client. He's trying to get her drunk. The jukebox is playing a song in Kabyle, all about the beauty of the women who live at the foot of the Jujura mountains.

The prostitute lets out a shrill scream, and all eyes in the bar focus onto her blouse. Her client is pawing her breasts, with his tongue hanging out. He tucks a banknote down her tight-fitting, low-cut dress. She laughs and pretends to give a little shiver. Majid puts a coin on the counter and signals to the barman that it's for his beer plus the old fellow's red wine. The old man finishes his drink in one gulp, and plunges one hand into the pocket of his long, dark overcoat. He pulls out a Basque beret which he places on his bald head. Majid takes his change and heads for the door.

The little old man follows him without a word. In the still of the night, the two men walk the length of rue des Compagnons. The old man walks in the middle of the road, taking short, quick steps, his hands buried in the large pockets of his overcoat. Suddenly a car comes up behind them, headlights blazing.

Majid takes the little man by the arm and brings him onto the pavement. The car passes. The young man and his father return to the middle of the street, since there are cars parked all along the pavement. Majid pulls out two cigarettes and lights both of them.

He gives one to his dad. The old man takes it with that same eternal expression in his eyes – a mixture of emptiness and distance. Majid watches for a moment and is moved by sudden pity and tenderness. His father used to work as a roofer. One day he fell from a roof, onto his head. He 'lost his head', as his wife puts it. And now she sees him as one more child in the family, always needing to be looked after. She washes him, dresses him, shaves him and gives him a bit of money for his cigarettes and the occasional glass of red wine.

'Your father was a fine man before his accident. A good man.' This is Malika's standard reproach to Majid. 'Not a layabout like you. If only you could be like your father was before his accident.'

But Majid's different from his dad. He's the same height, but more solidly built. These days he could pick his father up with one hand, the same way that his father used to pick up the kids when Majid was young. Majid remembers that. It's true, his dad was nice. He loved his kids. He dressed them up and spoiled them like a mother. And on Sundays, when the weather was good, he'd take them to the horse races – Maisons-Laffitte, Auteuil and Enghien. The kids loved that. They'd picnic in the woods, and then play football before going to the racetrack. They were a wonderful sight on Sunday mornings, each of the kids with their sandwiches under one arm and a plastic flask of water, or mint cordial, or grenadine, hanging from their waists. Their father marched ahead of them, and when the kids dawdled in front of some shop window, he'd hurry them along. They couldn't be late for the first race!

They took the bus the way that other people take a plane — with a sense of adventure. Malika stayed at home — after all, someone had to do the washing, the ironing and the housework. Anyway, she enjoyed having Sunday afternoons to herself.

These days, though, their father's adrift in a boat that has lost its sail. Majid sometimes thought that even if he ever managed to land somewhere, it would probably turn out to be a desert island.

Pat comes down the street to meet them, his hands in the back pockets of his jeans, walking like a cowboy who's about to wreck the local saloon. The bunch of keys at his waist jangles in time with his footsteps.

'Taking daddy home, are we?' he says, mockingly.

Then he goes, 'Ha!' like he does every time when he takes the piss out of someone and then doubles up laughing — 'Ha!'

The silence of the night is disturbed by the sound of a fire engine. Majid looks at Pat, who scratches his head and frowns:

'Funny how they always seem to arrive too late. . .'

Majid takes his dad by the arm and says:

'Come on, we're going round the other way.'

While they're skirting the estate, along by the motorway, Pat starts pulling faces at Majid's dad.

First he cocks a snook, then he sticks out his tongue, then he gives him two fingers, and so on, getting ruder all the time. The little old man is lost to the world, though, and doesn't react at all.

'Leave him alone,' says Majid, irritated.

'I'm not doing any harm. Just trying to get a smile out of him. Doesn't he ever laugh?'

'Your arsing around is hardly going to make him laugh. . .'

At this point Pat suddenly snatches the old man's beret and runs off with it. The old fellow stops dead in the middle of the street. He starts shouting, but like a dumb person:

'Mmmm. . . Ummm. . .!'

Majid runs after Pat.

'Give him back his beret, you shit!'

Pat is larking about with the beret on his head. Majid returns to his father, who is emitting shrill little cries and reaching out towards Pat. He stands there, rooted to the spot. Majid takes him by the arm again, to lead him forward. Nothing doing – the old man wants his beret back. He stamps his feet.

Once again, Majid pleads, 'Give it back to him, for fuck's sake.'

His father is still making his angry noises. Then he starts to cry, like a kid.

By now Majid is furious: 'Now look what you've done. You've started him crying.'

'Ha!' says Pat, and he comes back and tosses the beret to Majid. The old man pulls his beret on, stops crying, and sets off down the road again.

'You're really fucking stupid sometimes,' says Majid.

'Ouf!' says Pat, with an exaggerated shrug of his shoulders. 'Today's kids – you can't even have a laugh with them!'

That's one of his favourite phrases. Sometimes he adds: 'Young people are pathetic these days.'

As they near their apartment-block, they see a police car arrive with its blue lights flashing aggressively. The cops make for the parking-lot where firemen are struggling to douse the flames that are engulfing Jean-Marc's dad's car.

It's good entertainment.

Josette brings her son Stephane to Malika's flat, as she does every working day. She finds Malika busy dressing the kids for school. Stephane has more or less grown up in this flat, since Malika was his child-minder for the first three years of his life – in fact she still is, because Josette has to start at the factory very early in the morning. It's Malika who takes Stephane to school and brings him home in the evening. When she was minding him full-time, it brought in a bit of money, but now she does it for free. Particularly since she overheard Josette talking about redundancies. She doesn't like to ask questions, though.

It's time to give the little ones their breakfast. Stephane's joined in the others' games, and they're playing at the Three Musketeers, making a huge racket. Josette's already left for work.

Wearing a light, navy-blue mac and a scarf around her neck, she hurries along between rows of factories. Day is barely dawning over the suburbs. It's winter. 'Chousette', as Malika calls her in her heavily-accented French, finally reaches the bus stop. She waits in the shelter and lights a cigarette, glancing at her watch as she does so.

This is the hour of the immigrant worker – after the milkman and just before the dustman. Josette greets two Africans who join her at the bus stop, as they do every morning. They're late too. The bright neon panels of the bus shelter are an assault on their tired eyes. Josette's not wearing make-up. She doesn't usually bother, except maybe on special days like payday.

Since her divorce, she's tended to go to pieces. She's delicately built, like a slender green plant, but there's little colour in her cheeks and no hope in her eyes. The bus comes. She pulls out her bus pass. The two Africans let her on first. She sits in her usual place, at the back on the right, next to the window.

The bus cuts through the suburban night. This is Josette's life – every morning, every day, the same surroundings, with the driver calling out each stop in the tone of a waiter in a café ordering up a salami sandwich. And as the girls board the bus, the driver turns his head to watch them go by.

The bus seems not to be in a hurry. Josette rings the bell for the Pont de Clichy stop, and gets off. A gentle breeze tugs at her and she lowers her head and turns round in order to light yet another cigarette. She walks along the quayside, down by the Seine.

It's barely daylight. Josette's hunched silhouette melts into the darkness beneath the factory walls. She meets some of her workmates. They shake hands, with a barely audible 'Good morning', and as they reach the factory they hurry to get into the warm. About fifty of the girls gather round the coffee dispenser. They look weary, and talk in subdued voices, as if afraid that someone might overhear them.

In the middle of the shop floor there's a huge poster, announcing:

ALL-OUT STRIKE
NO SACKINGS!
OCCUPY THE FACTORY!

Josette blows on her coffee. She's standing among a group of women and listening to their comments before the morning's demonstration. On a long bench that runs the length of the workshop stand their sewing machines, the instruments of their labour, covered with sheets of navy-blue plastic to protect them from damp and dust.

Next to the wall are stacked boxes of material, waiting for the strong, nimble fingers of the girls who will come and empty them. These girls have three minutes in every two hours when they can go the toilet or smoke a cigarette. It's forbidden to smoke on the shop floor, in case it starts a fire. Now the boss is saying that there's an economic crisis and he's got to sack a third of his staff. The ones who will go are the girls who are taken on in peak periods but then dropped at the first sign of a downturn – single mothers for the most part, the ones who never go on strike, the ones who are most in need. Josette is one of those due to be made redundant. She's only been there for two years, which makes her more or less a new starter, and the new starters are the first in line for joining the queue at the job centre.

Pat and Majid had first run into each other at technical college – the university for working-class kids with no future. They'd already known each other for a fair while, but they'd been wary of each other until their second year at college, when they suddenly became good friends. The crazier you are, the more laughs you have. But this kind of relationship is weird. At the start – particularly when you're in the same class – the main thing governing the relationship is your fear of each other.

If there had been a fight between the two of them, the loser would inevitably have lost face with the rest of the class. Neither Pat nor Majid wanted this to happen. They preferred to act in tandem so that they could keep the upper hand over the others and show the teacher who was boss. It was a form of weakness, and they knew it – two weaknesses don't make a strength, but at least it reduces the fear.

They were soon identified as a pair of trouble-makers, but this didn't stop them hanging out with their classmates and involving them in all kinds of shady deals. They already had an extortion racket going with the younger kids. Majid did the best he could in class and tried to get at least halfway decent marks. Pat, however, was bottom of the class. Not at the back of the class, though, where the central heating was. No – right at the front, next to the teacher's raised desk, where it was harder for her to keep an eye on him. This was his place, and woe betide anyone else who tried to sit there, because one day, in between lessons, Pat had carved a hole in the front of the teacher's desk, so that he could sit and look at her legs. These voyeur sessions were the best moments of his week, and in the break he'd make the most of them:

'She was wearing blue knickers today. . . a bit transparent. . . you could see her black hair through them.'

He left his classmates salivating. If any of the other students managed to sneak up to the peep-hole, Pat would let him get an eyeful; then he'd give him a boot up the backside. The head of the student in question would bang against the desk, and the teacher would suddenly sit up in her chair. She must have known something was going on, but she never let on. She would scold Pat for being so mean to his classmates. Pat would defend himself:

'Well, they shouldn't get in my way.'

His classmate would go back to his desk rubbing his forehead, and the teacher never said a word about the hole. She must have found it amusing to give the lads a hard-on. As long as their minds were on sex, things were quieter in the classroom. . . When Pat was in a good mood, the whole class would be allowed a look through the hole. Furtively, cautiously, they'd approach the hole on all fours. Pat would decide the viewing rota. The

ensuing murmurings aroused the teacher's suspi-
cions. She'd pretend not to have noticed anything,
she'd spread her legs a little wider, and the lads
would return to their desks suitably aroused.

Some days, she'd camp it up a bit. She'd begin
her strip-tease routine before lessons even started.
She'd make sure that she was the first one to go up
the stairs; the boys would wait until she'd gone up
a few steps, then they'd follow behind her. This was
the only moment of silence in the whole day. She'd
climb the stairs nonchalantly, keeping close to the
outer banister, so that the little ones could get an
eyeful too, to compensate for the hours of boredom
that lay ahead of them. Her scanty knickers showing through her dress were a marvel, a challenge. A
smack in the face. A master-stroke. And the lads followed her as one, heads looking up, and all with the
same idea, the same mouth-watering desire. Three
flights like that, hardly daring to breathe. What
a turn-on! And Pat became positively angelic. He
looked like a choirboy following the priest with a
candle in his hands. He'd climb the stairs with his
head raised and his eyes fixed on the Holy Virgin
ahead. At times like these, you could push him and
not get hit in return. It was as if he was in a trance,
and his horizon was set at the precise point where
her knickers concealed the secrets of her sex. By the
time they reached the classroom, they all had their
heads filled with dreams and hopes, but only Pat
was able to continue the journey, with his eyes
glued to the hole in the front of the desk.

Pat and Majid didn't last long at the college –
but they set their mark on it before being sent back

to the concrete jungle. They weren't worried by the teachers or the college staff. The only thing that worried them was the boredom. Pat was hauled up before the college disciplinary board, but it made no difference. He just hated school, and that was that. He'd spend his days playing the hard man, and the best part of his day was lunch-time in the canteen.

Needless to say, Pat was head of the table, with Majid opposite him and three others down each side. A table for eight. There was no problem with the starters, because they were served in individual portions. But when Pat was hungry, seriously hungry, particularly when he hadn't been home the night before, God help the others at the table! Meat and vegetables were served together in one big tray. Pat would wait until Majid had served himself a generous portion; then he'd pull the tray over and with a sadistic snigger he'd spit into the food – a great gob of spit that came gurgling up from the depths. He'd wipe his lips with the back of his hand and then pass the tray to the younger pupils. Needless to say, none of them felt inclined to claim their helping.

'So – are you eating or not?' Pat would ask.

Nobody answered. Majid just sat and ate, without a word – another part of the routine. And the kids felt like throwing up.

So Pat would take the food back and eat straight out of the serving-tray. The others would nibble at a lump of bread, all the while keeping a protective hand on their desserts. Obviously, everyone tried to avoid eating at Pat's table, but there were only so many places to go round. Luckily there were always the first-years who hadn't yet learnt how to defend themselves. They sat in the empty chairs and prayed that the ogre wasn't too hungry.

The college authorities and the kids were both equally relieved when Pat and Majid were finally thrown out. It happened during a maths lesson – a subject which they found particularly baffling.

Pat used to boast that he had the biggest cock in the class. This used to irritate Majid, so on this particular day he decides to challenge him.

'Come on, then, let's measure them.'

They masturbate under the desk to give themselves a hard-on. The teacher's got his nose buried in a book, waiting for the students to finish their written test. There's silence in the room. Everyone else is working.

Pat takes the ruler and surreptitiously measures his cock. Then he murmurs in Majid's ear:

'Fifteen.'

Majid doesn't believe him. He looks at him accusingly:

'Liar!'

'I'm telling you.'

Majid measures his own cock:

'Fourteen and a half.'

'I've beaten you,' says Pat, proudly.

'You're lying, anyway.'

'You wait and see,' Pat retorts, putting the ruler on top of his cock again.

'Don't push the ruler, you'll make a hole in yourself.' says Majid.

'I'm not pushing. There – look – what does it say?'

'Fourteen. . . just under fourteen.'

'You can't see properly down there,' says Pat, uneasily.

Slighted and feeling humiliated, he puts his cock up on the desk and practically shouts:

'There you are – now measure it in the light!'

Majid doesn't budge. He folds his arms across his blank sheet of paper and watches in amusement as the teacher shouts at Pat, 'Right – you've gone too far this time, you little arsehole!' His face red with anger, he grabs Pat and drags him to the door.

'To the principal's office – at once!'

Pat breaks free, pushes the teacher away, and shouts:

'You wait, I'm going to get you. . .!'

Majid innocently zips up his fly.

'You too,' the teacher shouts. 'Go on – out!'

'Don't worry,' Pat shouts back. 'We wouldn't waste them on the likes of you.'

They joined each other outside, and went to sit on the steps of a block of flats. They felt like they were foreigners newly arrived in a country where everything moves very fast, newcomers who have to adapt to the demands, the style of life and the temperament of others in order to survive. You either pretend to follow the crowd, or you reject the system and turn your back on society. Because it wears you out when you go running after a carrot – especially when you know that the carrot's been rotten for a long time anyway. . .

'No point in busting a gut,' says Pat. 'We'll wait and see, and if nothing turns up, we can always fuck off somewhere.'

For them, college life is finished. No point in signing up for another. Once you've been thrown out by the Marguerites, you've had it. And people said: 'We warned you. . .'

And Pat answered: 'Who bloody cares!' And it was true – Pat didn't care – although occasionally he did have a twinge of nervousness about what the future might hold.

'What d'you say, Maj? Who gives a shit, eh?'

'Too right,' says Majid, not entirely convinced.

They laugh and slap hands. A gesture of true friendship. Together through thick and thin. After all, what have they got to be scared of? They don't even have a father to give them a good thrashing. . . Pat's dad had taken off with Marinette, a young girl from the estate. Everyone knew they'd had a scene together, but nobody ever expected that they'd run off together like a pair of love-birds. He'd taken off one morning on his way to work, with his cap on his head and his lunch-bag over his shoulder, and that was the last they'd heard of him.

Marinette was his neighbour on the third floor, and he'd been screwing her for a while. She had three kids and a lorry-driver husband. 'Big-boy' was how the truck-driver was known on the estate, a man with a head like a cockroach. The only time you ever used to see him was at weekends – that is, until his wife left him to go off with Pat's old man. Now he's around the place every day. He left his old trade and took a job in the town hall so that he could bring up the kids on his own. Marinette was fifteen years younger than her new boyfriend. Maybe she felt her sex was going to waste, what with her husband never being there.

The two lovers did a bunk. Dropped everything, without a thought for the future, and bade farewell to the concrete jungle. Pat had known that his dad was screwing Marinette. The old bastard used to laugh about it, boasting that the men in his family had balls. What he didn't know was that Pat had also screwed Marinette. . . a fact that he was rather proud of.

Anyway, which of the tenants cooped up in these

flats could swear that their partners were faithful
to them? The boredom, the routine and the longing
for a bit of excitement. You have to do something to
break the monotony, the drabness that gets hold of
you and begins to squeeze the life out of you, like
a giant octopus. The greyness enters your soul and
finally chokes you. In a sea of mediocrity, the least
mediocre is king. If you can screw your neighbour's
wife, it means you think you're smarter than he is,
because you've nicked his woman. And when you do
what you like, you're saying that you deserve better
than what you've got, and that you've the right to a
better life. And what about emotions and feelings?
No chance! The main thing is to fight the despair,
find something to believe in, no matter what it
takes. They find it in what looks like a secure haven
– a little hole with a bit of hair round it. Dozens
of them have taken off like this, running from the
greyness, abandoning their wives and children, and
the mother-in-law.

They run off with the first round, pink arse that
comes along, preferably young and still smelling of
pissy playground toilets. And they never return. You
never know whether this is because they're happier
somewhere else, or whether they're even worse off
and just don't dare come back to admit it.

Maybe they come back secretly and hide behind
the parked cars to watch their kids coming out of
school. They see the kids, pale and sad, holding each
other's hands, and they see how they've grown. The
prodigal's heart skips a beat. The children grow up
as part of the cement and concrete. They grow up
and they begin to take on the characteristics of

concrete: they're dry and cold and hard, to all appearances indestructible – but they've got hidden cracks. You see it clearest when they cry – they cry like a little kid when someone's stolen his marbles and he's got no older brother to defend him. It splits your skin, it catches you unawares, it runs down like one of the rivers on the geography maps that they try to drum into your head at school, enough to put you off travel for life. It's like the cracks in the concrete – right from when you're a kid. . . cracks in your heart, in your face. They get wider over time, and deeper. They expand like a lake. . . an indelible scar. . . a great gash. . . right down to your guts. And it all comes out when times are hard, when your body and soul are tired and simply can't take the pace. These cracks come back, and they eat into your soul. If you don't do something about them, you find yourself swallowed up, swollen, stifled by a desire to scream, a desire to explode.

The main thing is to show nothing, because one moment's weakness and it's all over town and everyone's talking about you. No tears. Don't cry – never! Just store it all up, and wait, wait forever, with perhaps a small hope of being able to reconcile yourself with your life. Because if you don't, the explosion will come, and it will come like the awakening of a volcano that has long planned its revenge for everything that it's had to endure. It suddenly expels the sleeping energy that has been brooding in its guts. It turns from good to bad. It turns destructive, and that means violence. . . a refusal. . . a refusal to let yourself be silenced. . . a refusal to allow yourself to be swallowed up. When you try to break the silence and the self-destructiveness, violence takes the upper hand, and you turn savage. You never recover from the concrete. It never leaves you. It's there, like a weight, in your movements, your voice, your eyes, the way you speak. . . right down to your fingertips. On your arm it translates into a bottle-green tattoo of a four-leafed clover, a rose, and a dedication to 'Mother — Forever'. It follows you everywhere. And because you were born into it, it will never give you up.

The concrete has a smell, too. The sort of smell that lingers at the back of your throat. And how do you get rid of it? People have tried everything. . . alcohol, drugs. . . It doesn't go away. It clings to you like a caterpillar on a branch. If you try to choke it, you just end up dead. The taste in your throat demands to have its say, and it doesn't let go until the good Lord has had his way with you.

The concrete doesn't sing, it screams – howls despair, like wolves in the forest, in the snow, without the strength to dig a hole to die in. They wait there like idiots, waiting to see if someone will get them out. They wait like the children of the concrete. People give them a wide berth, because they're scary. When you have to deal with them, it's best to destroy them outright, separate them out and pick them off one at a time. Because in packs they attack. They are dangerous.

Josette's come to collect her kid from Malika's. She's later than usual. Stephane's sitting on Amaria's knee on the bed in the living-room. The flat smells of *chorba*, the hot, spicy soup which, as Malika tells her offspring when they refuse to eat it, is good for killing winter germs.

Majid's on his way down to find his dad, and meets Josette in the hall. They say hello, without stopping to talk. Just a 'Good evening' and a friendly smile.

Malika asks Josette to stay for supper.

'It's a good hot soup.' No. Josette has no appetite for food – or for life, either.

'For the little one's sake,' says Malika.

'No. I'm tired.'

Amaria gets up to lay the table. Stephane puts his coat on and looks for his school bag.

'What's happening about the strike?' Malika asks.

'Still going on. We had a union meeting this evening – that's why I was late. . .'

Josette kneels down in front of her kid, buttons his coat, arranges his scarf, and then continues in a tired voice.

'I reckon it's all over now. We'll be sacked, and
that's that. . .'

Amaria chips in:

'All of you?'

'No. Just some of us. Last in, first out.'

'What are you going to do?'

'Look for a job,' Josette replies, shaking her head
as if to say, 'It's going to be hard finding one.'

Stephane goes to kiss Malika goodbye. Malika
raises a warning finger:

'Be a good boy this evening, your mummy's
tired.'

The kid pays no attention. Josette smiles. A sad
smile.

Malika repeats her invitation to stay for supper.
She makes it clear that Josette is one of the family,
and that she thinks of Stephane as one of her own.
Josette believes her. Malika is a good woman –
warm and generous – and she knows how much
she owes her – but this evening her heart's just not
in it.

She wants to be alone in her little apartment right
at the heart of the tower-block. . . alone with her
loneliness.

She makes herself a ham sandwich. Stephane's
not hungry. He's been eating chocolate cakes at
Malika's. He's finished his homework, with Mehdi's
help – Mehdi or Amaria usually help him with his
schoolwork. Josette watches the news on TV while
the little one lies on the floor and plays with his toy
cars. He pretends that two lorries have just crashed:
'Nyaaa. . . bonk!' His hand indicates a cloud of dust
rising.

Someone's talking about unemployment on the television. Josette clears the table and puts the washing-up in the sink. She presses her nose against the window.

The city smothers lonely souls. Josette is without hope. Her body is gone – she leaves it just enough of a breathing space to keep it going, to preserve it, for even harder nights to come, for the sleepless nights of fear and loneliness. You pull the curtains to hide this fear, this loneliness, and you console yourself that there's always someone more lonely than you. Find some way of giving yourself courage. . .

The kid's playing with his racing cars.

His mum goes to undress in the bathroom. She takes off her tights and runs her hands over her thighs as if to massage them. Her breasts are two little pointed mounds. She combs out her long brown hair and it caresses her shoulders as it falls. The comb traces long, shiny furrows in her hair, and carries away a few strands in its teeth.

In the living-room there's been an accident. Stephane calls out the ambulance. It comes, complete with a wailing siren: 'Nee-naa, nee-naa, nee-naa.'

Josette puts the comb back on the shelf of the bathroom cabinet, next to the strip of contraceptive pills. She takes the strip and checks the date to see when she last took one. It was a Tuesday. But when? She can't remember the month. She sees her body in the mirror. She has the feeling that she's fading. . . that she's somehow turning lifeless. . .

She has no sex life now, and she worries that her body's lost the knack. She runs her hand over her thighs and up over her breasts. She's got goose pimples. She's had no men in her life since the divorce. She's not felt the need for sex, or the desire. Except just once, after she'd been to a friend's wedding.

She'd overdone it a bit on champagne. That night, she'd gone to bed with a headache and a feeling that she wanted to make love. She'd masturbated between the sheets.

This was the last time she'd felt her body, the last time she'd felt that quivering at the base of her spine. She remembers that time, and how she'd found the heat of passion all on her own. After the final groan, as she lay there in a haze, with her arms crossed on the pillow, she'd been startled to find that she was crying. Not tears of pleasure after orgasm, but tears of regret, of loneliness and a sense of loss. A sense of emptiness, just like this evening. A feeling of marking time in a world that won't wait for you, a world that is speeding past. If you miss the train, it leaves you standing on the platform, dry-mouthed and forgotten. And when you've a kid on your hands, that's hard.

What's even harder is when the kid occasionally asks after his dad. What do you tell him? He sits there, picking his nose, with a big question in his little round eyes. What do you tell him. . .?

'Stop picking your nose!'

The kid gets the message and returns to the safety of his game.

She puts on her dressing-gown and goes to join Stephane in the living-room. To get away from the mirror.

Solange jumps as Pat puts his hand on her shoulder. She spins round.

'Did I frighten you?'

'You caught me off guard a bit,' she replies, in her rough, Parisian accent. She puckers up her eyes and grimaces as she speaks. How old is she really? Twenty-eight, maybe? Alcohol has dried her out, made her ugly. Her lank, greasy hair falls onto her shoulders like the mane of a horse that has been rolling in the mud. She trails from bar to bar — drunk from morning to night. And she's been laid by every man on the block. 'Had more men than I've had hot dinners,' as Pat would say. She'll sell her body for a lager or a bottle of cheap wine. Her bloke's in nick, on a long stretch. A serious villain, by all accounts. She's got two kids, who are looked after by her mother-in-law, a crazy old lady who blasts off with a shotgun if anything so much as moves in front of her door after dark. She usually has one of her kids trailing after her, skinny and grubby, like a little dog. When she's drunk and collapses in the gutter, it's the kid who has to pick her up. He holds his stick of liquorice between his teeth and helps his mother up in his arms, as if it's just another part of life's routine. Sometimes when she's drunk too much, she's too heavy for him, so he sits by the wall next to her, waiting for her to finish vomiting and ranting. And as he waits he watches the other kids as they play in the sand pit.

On this particular evening, she's still more or less upright. Not completely plastered yet.

'You coming with us?'

'Hey! Where to?'

'How'd you fancy coming along for a bit of nookie?'

'Well, get a load of you, eh! You've got a nerve!'

'Well? You coming?'

'OK. I'm game. But I'm a bit off form today.' Solange's kid follows them. Majid gives the boy a weary look and pushes him back.

'You stay here and wait for us,' he says, stroking the kid's hair.

The child holds his hand out like a beggar. Majid calls to Pat, who pulls out a coin and hands it to him. Solange tells the boy, 'Say thank you to the man. . .' But the little one's already halfway up the street on his way to the baker's.

'Doesn't hang about, does he!' she said. 'That kid'll go far.'

'Just like his dad,' says Pat.

'What did you say?'

Solange is not amused.

'I mean, his dad was a good runner too,' Pat replies.

'I thought you meant something else,' she says, as she struggles to keep up with them.

She pauses for a good sniff.

'Yes, he could give a good wallop, too, my old man.'

The three of them head off down the road towards the docks, along by the market gardens which will soon be flattened by a motorway.

Acres of wasteland and mounds of garbage, and a little breeze that just ruffles your hair. They reach the edge of a gypsy camp. There's a scorching smell of burning rubber that tears at your lungs. And there's Manitas, the gypsy, with the hot copper, straight out of the fire. And his dogs, tugging at their chains and barking fit to raise the dead. Their arrival has not gone unnoticed. The whole of the gypsy family turns and stares at them.

'You mustn't look at their women,' Pat whispers to Majid. 'Try to look like we're just passing through.'

But Majid can't take his eyes off the gypsy women. He thinks they're amazing, the way they're always dressed in technicolour like an arrangement of Japanese flowers. They wear long, brightly-coloured skirts – a blinding yellow with bright pink roses. And when they walk, they look as if they're dancing. . . gliding. . . graceful and relaxed. . . like swans on a lake. As Majid watches them, he wonders how on earth such beautiful women can have ended up out here in the middle of nowhere, surrounded by filthy pots and pans. If he had his way, he'd haul them off to a fancy patisserie, and he'd make them a bed among the coloured candies – the round white ones, the blue oval ones and the red flat ones that he remembered from when he was a kid with his mouth watering at the shop window.

They're always dressed to kill. A ring on each finger, golden bracelets on their wrists and big, brass ear-rings that brush against their shoulders every time they move. You yearn to get close to them, just to smell their scent. Their gestures don't say a lot – everything is in the voice – but you can read their emotions, or their tiredness, in the depths of their big, dark eyes.

Majid's not particularly interested in the gypsy menfolk. Most of the time they go around in shirt-sleeves – green check shirts, by preference – and bottle-green ties. The head of the family looks like a bouncer in a not very successful nightclub. A Clark Gable moustache and built like the side of a house. He smokes a clumsily-rolled cigarette that he holds between his greasy fingers. When the cigarette goes out, he reaches for the bottle of cheap wine sitting in the shade of his old, black Peugeot 403. He chases the fly off the rim and takes a swig. And there he sits, on the steps of his caravan, holding the bottle on his knee as if it were a crystal ball.

Majid feels the urge to say hello, just to hear their accents or the sound of their voices in reply, but he doesn't dare. Manitas comes towards them, bare-chested, with his face and hands blackened by the smoke of the bonfire. Arms akimbo, he bars their way like a customs officer. He looks furious. When he comes into town, he's a small, creeping sort of man, but here, on his own territory, he's the man. 'What the fuck are you doing here?' he bawls.

'Just passing through,' says Pat.

'Find some other way through.'

'Keep your hair on, Manitas. . . you know us, don't you?'

'What did you call him?' asks Solange.

'Manitas.'

'Like the Spanish singer? How funny!' And she laughs out loud. Majid mutters in her ear:

'No, the thing is, the singer's a gypsy too. That's how come they've got the same name.'

'Yeah,' says Pat. 'I bet with a name like that he gets to screw all the little gypsy girls. . .'

'Anyway,' says Manitas, 'I don't want the likes of you coming through here.'

Pat and Majid give each other a meaningful look that says a lot about the welcome Manitas can expect next time he decides to venture onto their patch. It'll be VIP treatment everywhere he goes – but the gypsy doesn't seem to get the message, and continues threatening them:

'I thought I told you, fuck off!'

The man's beginning to get on Majid's nerves. 'What are you on about? Go burn your copper and leave us alone.'

'Copper?' Manitas is upset now. 'Where've you seen any copper, eh, you little arsehole? I get it! You've come here to spy on me – I knew it!'

'No,' says Pat, all sweetness and light, 'No, not at all. . . As far as we're concerned, your copper doesn't even exist. We're on our way to the docks. . .'

'All right, then — fuck off!' the gypsy shouts, making a sudden move. 'Or I'll set the dogs on you.'

'I thought you loved your animals – you're surely

not going to wear the poor bastards out running after us, are you?'

The three of them move off, laughing among themselves, but not too loud, because the dogs are still barking behind them.

The gypsy returns to his fire, cursing under his breath. Not much taller than a bar-stool, but mean with it. Not a man to mess with.

They walk through the long wild grass by the side of the disused railway line, to the hostel where the immigrant workers live. Solange complains endlessly.

'How much further is it?' she asks. 'I've got stones in my shoes.'

As she walks, she treads on the hem of her long, crumpled Indian skirt.

'We're almost there,' Majid reassures her. 'Look, those yellow huts over there, behind the crane. . .'

They slide down the railway embankment, holding on to the long grass as they go. Solange comes down on her backside.

The barracks consist of rows of prefabs on a stretch of stony, dusty wasteland, which turns into a mud-patch in winter. These barracks are run by local employers, and they house workers from North Africa and the Mediterranean. They live here like animals, excluded from the normal life of the city, stuck between the roadworks on the motorway, the railway line and the harbour, in a work-camp surrounded by a wire fence.

Pat heads for the first hut. He walks round it and looks in. Not a soul to be seen. At the second hut he hears a noise, and beckons to Pat and Solange to join him.

Majid knocks at the hut door.

Pat pushes Solange gently forward as the door opens to reveal an ill-shaven man of about forty years of age, who looks like he's just got off the train from Lisbon.

'What d'you want?' he says, and he glares at them. Pat smiles and points to Solange.

'See her?' he says, ruffling Solange's hair. 'She's my sister. You like her. . .?'

The Portuguese doesn't know what to say. He undresses Solange with his eyes, and then turns and calls into the hut:

'Joachim!'

Joachim is a big, red-faced man with hair the colour of corn. 'How much?' asks Joachim.

'Fifty francs,' Pat replies.

'You must be kidding!' says Redface.

'Very well, poppet,' says Solange, making a big bow. 'We'll be seeing you. . .'

'We'll try next door,' says Majid.

But Joachim's had second thoughts:

'Thirty.'

Solange jumps at the offer. Not surprising, seeing that she usually gets laid for a packet of cigarettes. By the time Pat and Majid have opened their mouths to say something, she's already in the hut.

'OK,' she says. 'You're on. But you only get one go each.'

The men follow her.

'Pull the curtains in here,' she tells them.

She's already pulling off her knickers, as she

eyes the porn pictures that are pinned to the wall between the bunk beds. One of the men is smiling and is clearly embarrassed. She shows off her sex:

'It's the real thing,' she says, as she pulls up her dress. 'It'll be cash in advance, though.'

The men hurriedly dig out the money and place it on a little table in the middle of the room. One of them asks Pat and Majid to leave.

Solange wants one of the lads to stay, but the men won't have it. In the end, they all go out, because the little fat one wants to screw alone, and in the dark.

'You don't want us to see your tiny prick, eh?' is Pat's parting jibe as he leaves the hut.

The man doesn't reply.

They smoke a cigarette outside with the other Portuguese. He is impatient.

'Right,' says Majid. 'I'm off to see if there's anything doing in the other huts.' It takes them a full hour to do the round of all the men who want a screw. The impoverished sex lives of immigrant workers make a good little earner, and in no time at all they've collected a tidy sum.

Solange is completely drunk, not least because she's been asking each of her clients for a beer. A quick piss in the sink, and off to the next hut. Pat keeps an eye on his watch – five minutes per customer and not a minute more. All goes well until one of the residents starts shouting abuse at them and accusing Solange of having the clap.

'You filthy little pimps,' he shouts, as he chases them from the camp. He threatens that next time he'll call the police. And his final words echo after them as they go: 'We're not bloody savages.'

They set off home again, this time bypassing the gypsy camp. Pat counts out the money as he goes and divides it into three. Solange is complaining of a pain in her kidneys.

'Hardly surprising,' says Pat, 'when you've been screwed by a bunch of animals like that. You'll get a good night's sleep, though. . .'

You make it sound like I'm a machine. Don't you think I've got feelings? It makes me want to throw up, you know.'

'Didn't you enjoy it?' asks Pat, sounding surprised.

Solange stopped, swayed a bit, gave him a pained look, and said:

'I've not had any pleasure out of it for years. All I feel is their sperm running down my thighs.'

All of a sudden she has tears in her eyes. The hand that is holding her money drops to her side and hangs there limply as her head sags forward and her hair covers her face.

'I don't feel anything any more. . . whatever I'm doing. . . And when it all gets to me, I just want to die. . .'

She stands tearfully in the middle of the road.

Majid's decency gets the better of him, and he offers her his share of the money.

She refuses. He is annoyed and doesn't know what to say.

She sniffs, and bursts into tears again.

Pat lets out a sigh of irritation. He doesn't like emotional scenes. He's itching to get back to town.

Majid is still insisting on giving Solange his share of the money.

'I suppose you think that'll make me happy,' she says.

He stuffs the notes into her blouse.

'Come on, stop crying. This is for your kids.'

Pat is annoyed. He wants to keep his share of the money, but in the end he hands it over. Then he turns to Majid and grunts:

'All that effort for nothing. . .!'

'So what? We can't just leave her to starve, can we?'

'Can't you see she's just turning on the waterworks?'

Solange raises her head and holds out her arms. She kisses Pat on both cheeks. When Pat's like this, with his shoulders hunched so that you can't see his ears above the collar of his bomber-jacket, it means he's in a bad mood. Solange didn't notice, though. He could do without being kissed. He pulls a face, because the girl's breath isn't the sweetest in the world. Then he sets off down the street, walking in front of Majid, as his way of saying that this time they really have blown it.

Majid lets himself be kissed too. 'Thank you,' said Solange. 'At least you two are nice to me. It's not true when people say that young people are no good. You've just proved it. I won't forget it.'

Pat laughs out loud. Majid lets himself be kissed a second time. The smell of her breath reminds him of Madeleine.

Madeleine was a plump little Breton girl with pink cheeks, who lived on the estate with her parents. By the age of fourteen she had already deflowered most of the boys on the estate. She had no problems finding partners for sex, but they tended to like it short and sharp, on account of the fact that she had bad breath. She would go down to one of the basements with two or three lads at a time, and they'd do it on top of an old packing case.

The girl wasn't quite right in the head. She'd let them get on with it, and sometimes, by the time the last one was finishing, she might even start to get some enjoyment out of it. The boys would queue up with their cocks in their hands, watching the one who was on the job. They'd roll her over and roll her over again; they'd feel her breasts, and they'd learn something about the female sex organs. Madeleine liked the physical contact; there can't have been a lot of love in her family.

On one occasion, Pat happened to be on the scene, together with Majid. He took a look at her vagina, examining it closely as if to find what it was at the bottom of that hole that 'gives the chicks pleasure'. When he'd finished, he gave his opinion.

'That thing there, above the hole,' he indicated to his pals, 'like an elephant's ears, that's the clitoris.'

Majid laughed.

'What's so funny?' Pat asked, annoyed that anyone should mock his expertise.

'I'm not laughing about what you said. Ha, ha! It was just the bit about the elephant. Do you remember that time at school, when the teacher asked you the name of an animal beginning with N, and you said a nelephant? Ha, ha! And then he hit you. . .!'

Pat pretended to laugh too, but he was not amused.

This arrangement with Madeleine lasted for a long time.

The lads would get a screw at least once a week, and there were plenty of them. It lasted till the day that Bengston got the clap. At first he was bragging about it. Then it was painful to piss. And by the end it was excruciating. Everyone panicked and shut themselves in the toilets to take a look at their cocks. It turned out that five of them had caught it.

'It's nothing,' said Pat. 'Just a dose of clap. Love's revenge. The way they cure it is that the nurse cuts your cock open and blows down it to get rid of the germs. You get an ace hard-on. Mind you, it can be a bit painful – but it's nothing compared with cancer of the left testicle. . .'

He continued in this vein, scaring the life out of them.

Bengston was more scared than any of them. He

spent the whole day searching for Madeleine, cursing as he went. 'That'll teach you to go dipping your wick in a sewer,' Thierry told him, with the air of a great thinker. Pat was not amused.

'How do you know Maddie's a sewer, eh, dumbo? Have *you* ever screwed her?'

'Yes, I did, once. . .'

'Well it's a good thing our Maddie's there, because you're so fucking ugly that if it wasn't for her, you'd still be a virgin now. Maybe she has got bad breath, but she still does a better blow-job than your sister.'

Anyone else would have got his teeth knocked out, but Thierry was scared of Pat. 'My sister would never screw with a rat like you.'

Pat takes a drag on his cigarette. Then, with a vengeful smile, he plays his trump card:

'What's more, your sister swallows as well. . . You ask her if she still wears those little blue Petit Bateau knickers.'

That evening, Thierry waited for his younger sister as she came out of school and gave her a beating she would never forget. His honour vindicated, Thierry felt part of the gang again. And that was the last they ever saw of Madeleine – her parents sent her to the country to stay with her grandparents. To save her from the clutches of the inner city.

Just in time, too, because Balou, one of the lads from Dahlia House, was talking about putting Madeleine on the game – with a figure like hers, she'd have coined it in. This Balou was a menace. Majid, Pat and the others tended to avoid him. One night he had turned up in front of Acacia

House extremely drunk. The gang was hanging out as usual, when he suddenly appeared round the corner. They started making fun of how drunk he was, but then he suddenly pulled out a gun and fired a shot in the air. Everyone dived for cover, like athletes off the starting blocks, and Balou fell about laughing. Then he left, happy that at last he'd made someone sit up and take notice. All the lights went on in people's windows. This was his moment of triumph, and he was cock-a-hoop. Another time he'd come flashing it round the clubhouse. This was before they'd shut down the Youth Club. The lads were gathered round the table football and the ping-pong table, when they heard the sound of a car horn in the street.

Jean-Marc was the first to reach the window. The sight that greeted him was a black car with out-of-town number plates, parked just inside the Youth Club entrance, with its headlights blazing. Pat's eyes opened wide when he saw it. He opened his mouth, blew out his cheeks and spat on the ground: 'Jesus! Get this for a car!'

'It's Balou,' said Jean-Marc. 'Will you look at that motor!'

Balou had been off the scene for ages. How come he'd popped up now? He must have flipped! It was obviously a hire-car, and he'd covered all the windows with banknotes. Real banknotes. Big denomination notes, too. Stuck all over the windscreen. It gave Majid goose-pimples to see them. Pat was sweating visibly. They circled the car, pressing their hands against the windows and laughing nervously among themselves. And there was Balou, in the driving seat, looking like God Almighty. Dressed in a hand-tailored suit, with a red carnation in his buttonhole, a cigar, and cuff links. He played the scene for all it was worth. With a half-smile on his lips, he stared straight ahead of him, like the bad guy in a western. The gang circled the car, in a mixture of awe and amazement. Slapping hands. It was a good feeling – they were celebrating the fact that one of their number had finally made it. And they were impressed. There was a girl sitting on the back seat. Blond hair and curls. She was smoking a long, slim cigarette with a gold tip that was marked with red lipstick. She had a distant look in her eyes that seemed to ask what the hell she was doing stuck here with these lunatics. The lunatics, for their part, were rocking the car and banging on the windows, trying to make the money fall off. But every time a note came unstuck, Balou picked it up, licked it and stuck it back on the window.

The chick had her blouse unbuttoned, revealing small, firm breasts. Pat couldn't take his eyes off her. That fucking Balou – he'd planned this down to the last detail. He must have lain awake day and night dreaming of this moment. It was a great performance. The girl glanced at Pat and he smiled back, stupidly, like a native seeing his own reflection in a mirror. Balou wound down his window a little, and the gang gathered round. Without a word, he peeled off one of the banknotes from the windscreen, set light to it with a gold cigar lighter, and then lit his cigar with it – a showman's gesture that was slow, deliberate, and obviously rehearsed.

He put out the flame by crushing the banknote in his hand, blew the ash into the faces of his former pals crammed in at the window, and then threw the remains of his five-hundred-franc note out of the window. Bengston picked up what was left of it, and everybody laughed. Not Balou, though.

The show wasn't over yet. He turned to the girl in the back, gestured from left to right with his forefinger, and she spread her legs. Balou repeated the gesture, as if to say 'more', and she spread her legs even more. He switched his cigar to the other hand and lifted her short skirt up over her stomach.

Pat stared at her sex, asleep like a baby between her thighs. A shaved woman's sex, like he'd dreamed of since he was a kid. You're boss, Balou, he thought to himself. And then out loud, 'Jeez!'

He'd planned it all out in advance, remembering our fantasies as kids and the conversations we used to have down in the basement. He'd come with a chick with the kind of pussy we'd dreamed of in the playground. One up on the lads, without a doubt! Bengston giggled nervously and Pat wiped the condensation that his panting breath had made on the windows. Balou threw his cigar out. Nobody stooped to pick it up. He was mildly annoyed – he'd have enjoyed that. But the gang had their minds on something else. Thierry was flapping his hand in the air like he'd singed his fingers, as if to say, 'Shaved! I mean to say, for fuck's sake. . .!!'

Majid made as if to grab one of Balou's banknotes through the open window. Balou nodded at him, as if to say, 'Go ahead.' He put his finger on a button on the dashboard, and nodded to Majid again.

'Don't think so. . .' said Majid, 'I don't trust you.'

From the slightly sadistic smile on Balou's lips, it was obvious what would have happened.

The gang pretended to laugh, but in fact they found the whole scene unnerving. It was as if the maestro wasn't quite right in the head. One of the banknotes came unstuck, fell like a leaf, and landed on the gearstick. Balou picked it up, licked it like it was an ice cream, and was about to stick it back on the glass when he changed his mind and handed it to Thierry without so much as looking at him. Thierry thanked him, and then asked:

'Where did you get it, Balou?'

Balou thought for a minute, gave a mental touch to his image, and said:

'I suppose you want me to get my gun out again. . .'

He put his hand into his jacket. The gang shrank back. Balou burst out laughing, shoved the car into gear, and drove off with his tyres squealing.

'I tell you, if I was that girl, I'd have the willies, hanging round with a creep like that,' said Thierry, as he wiped the banknote on his jacket.

'You jealous, or what?' said Majid.

'He's certainly got style,' Pat concluded.

And they returned to the table-tennis table with their heads full of adventure. That was the last time anyone saw Balou in the area. There was a rumour that he was pimping in Barbès, and even a rumour that if anyone wanted a screw they should go and see him, because it was free for his pals.

'He's done OK for himself,' thought Majid as he pushed open the Youth Club door.

He thought of what had brought Balou to where he was now. It was as if it was all laid down in advance, as if it was the only path he could have taken, as if he'd become what he was supposed to become. It had probably all started when Balou had been thrown out of school at an early age when they found him extorting money from his classmates.

As a result, at the age of fourteen he was already out on the streets having to fend for himself. His dad had sent him to work for a miserly old pastrycook, who had him working upwards of fourteen hours a day. He would get home in the evenings, worn out, after having walked halfway across the western suburbs of Paris, with a little packet of cakes under his arm for his brothers and sisters. There were nine children in the family. Their father ran a café. He had left them and gone to live with a girl he'd picked up in a bar. He still liked to play the good father, and came to see them occasionally, but he never left them any money.

Their mother was finding it impossible to cope.

Balou no longer even joined the lads for a game of football. He was so tired on Sundays that he'd sleep in all day.

Then, one evening, he decided he'd had enough. He came home with his little packet under one arm, as usual – only this time it contained the takings from the till. He was now a wanted man. The police, the pastrycook and his own father were all out looking for him. He was out celebrating with his pals, and the drinks were on him. Brilliant! The party lasted for four days – till his dad finally got his hands on him. He tied him up, locked him in the bathroom and thrashed him till he drew blood. Then he took his belt to the mother, and beat her too, because she'd brought the kid up wrong. Balou ended up in borstal, and the ageing ex-wife was divorced and sent back to Tunisia.

Then the father sent for a young girl from the country, a poor kid from the mountains, and he married her. She spoke no French. Her job was to look after the kids, but none of them spoke Arabic either.

At the age of seventeen, after several spells in borstal, Balou returned. He took things easy for a while, keeping out of trouble, until the day when one of his sisters caught him screwing his step-mother. It was his youngest sister. She was so shocked that she screamed. Balou came all over the sheets. Since the old man couldn't perform, the young mother had taken up with the step-son. Once his father found out, Balou never set foot inside the flat again. His step-mother was put on the first boat back home, and the kids were dumped on the Welfare.

Josette wanders the streets of Paris with a newspaper under her arm, open at the job vacancies section. She has spent hours on buses and trains travelling to places that look promising, only to draw a blank every time. Round about midday she's overcome by tiredness. She buys herself a chocolate croissant and sits on a bench to eat it. A few pigeons gather round her, waiting for her to throw them crumbs, which she does. She feels like taking her shoes off, but doesn't like to, not in the street. Her feet are hurting; next time, she tells herself, she won't wear high heels. But you have to look presentable when you're looking for work. Most important of all, don't wear trousers. Personnel managers are usually scruffy dressers themselves, but when you apply for a job they still feel they have the right to criticize your appearance. And when you apply by post, they always ask you to send a photo, so's they can see if the girls look kissable, and so's they can make sure you're not a West Indian with a French name – even though the French West Indies is supposed to be part of France. . . at least, at election time. Bengston knows the score. He only hangs out with the Arab kids. Like he says:

'Even if some of the West Indian politicians have sold out, the West Indies are not for sale!'

And he gives two fingers to the world.

Josette takes the train from the Gare Saint Lazare.

All afternoon she's been doing the rounds of factories out in the suburbs, but she's still not downhearted. She's tried the supermarkets too, and the garages. . .

She keeps repeating to herself, 'I must find a job. . . I must find a job. . .'

She returns home when the brief winter daylight runs out. She picks up Stephane from Malika's, and at the same time asks her for a bit of bread, because she's forgotten to call in at the baker's. Malika looks concerned: 'Are you all right for money?'

'Yes – I just forgot to call at the baker's. I'm OK for shopping, apart from that. . .'

'Won't you stay and eat something, Josette?'

'No, I've got to be going. I've got things to do.'

Malika's not happy. Josette takes Stephane's hand and gets ready to leave. The boy lets out a Tarzan yell in the corridor – a trick he must have picked up in the playground.

Josette and her son have barely arrived home when there's a ring at the door. It's the kid's father. Josette lets him in. He's caught her off guard. Yet again she's forgotten that it's Friday – the day when the kid's dad comes to pick him up for the weekend.

Stephane's not ready yet. He kisses his dad, as if he's just arrived home from work, like in the old days. He tugs him by the hand to show him his colouring book.

'Everything OK?' asks the ex-husband.

'Yes, fine,' she replies.

He's a sporty type, about thirty years of age, with short-cropped hair, a dark red shirt and cord trousers. It's obvious from his face that he's the hard, secretive type: a man of few words. Josette gets some clothes ready for Stephane. Then she remembers – it's a bank holiday.

Two days without her kid. . . it's going to be hard.

Stephane's dad lifts him up, and picks up the bag of clothes.

'Are you coming, too, mum?'

'No. . .'

'Why don't you come too. . .?'

'I can't. I've got work to do.'

The father slips out of the door and calls the lift.

Josette leans back against the wall and shuts her eyes. Her body slides down the wall and slips to the floor. She rests her head on her knees; her long hair hides her face; she sniffs. Suddenly she gets up and rushes into her bedroom. She emerges with a bottle in her hand. Hurriedly she puts on her shoes and runs down the service stairs.

Stephane's already sitting in the back seat of his dad's car. There's a woman sitting in front. The kid looks at the woman's auburn hair. He leans over, trying to see her face. She turns round and smiles at him. She's older than his mother, and wears elegant make-up. Stephane is intimidated by her, and lowers his eyes. His dad settles himself at the wheel and puts on his safety belt. The kid stands up, looks at the woman again, bursts into tears and puts his arms round his dad's neck.

'What's up, Steph?' his dad asks.

The kid cries and buries his face in his father's back. Josette comes out of the flats and pretends not to notice the brunette. She takes the bottle over to the driver's side of the car.

'If he starts coughing in the night, give him a spoonful of this and raise his head with a pillow. . .'

Stephane calls out, 'Mum!'

Josette reaches through and strokes the little one's cheek.

'What's the matter?' she asks, with a lump in her throat.

By now he's crying his heart out, as if he's sinking, drowning. . .

Josette opens the rear door and picks him up. She hugs him close.

The kid's arms aren't long enough to hug his mum as he wants to, so he buries his face in her jumper. The car drives off.

The next morning finds Pat and Majid coming out of the job centre looking glum.

'Waste of time going back there. Never got anything for us.'

'Ought to check it out, though.'

The two friends head off in the direction of the station.

'You got a cigarette?' Pat asks a girl who happens to cross their path.

'Last one in the packet.'

They share it.

'Tell you what. . .' says Pat. 'Let's visit my mum at work. I'll ask her to lend me ten francs.'

'I bet she gives you an earful.'

'Specially 'cos my sister's working.'

'Working?'

'Sure. Don't know where, but she's working.'

'Your mum must be happy.'

'You're kidding. All I get is "Your sister's out at work and all you do is sit around all day. . . blah. . . blah. . . blah. . .!" I just tell them to fuck off, the pair of them.'

'What about your dad? Any news?'

'I've no idea where he is, but as far as I'm concerned he can stay there and leave us alone.'

When they reach Asnières, they pass through the main gate of the truck factory and head straight for the canteen. It's a huge area, that echoes with the clatter of knives and forks as the kitchen staff lay the tables. Majid waits at the door while Pat goes to find his mum among the girls in their white caps and orange blouses.

It's almost lunch time as Pat zigzags between the tables to find her. She's surprised to see him. She leaves off pushing her trolley. Majid toys with his lighter, smiling to himself, because he knows that Pat's about to get it from his mum. Coming to see her here is a provocation, especially since he's come to ask her for money. She looks older than her years, worn out by a life of hard work and disappointment; her face is pale and her dishevelled hair is only partly hidden by her cap.

Even from a distance, Majid can see that the poor woman's unhappy as she waves her arms about. It's also obvious that Pat's piling on the pressure. His mother starts threatening him and wagging her finger at him. She must be saying something like, 'This is the last time! Next time you can go and get a job!' He'll be saying: 'Honest, mum, I'm going on an electricians' training course, and I'll be getting paid – that's what they said at the job centre. I've even filled in the form. I've just got to wait for an appointment.'

'You dirty bastard!' Majid thinks to himself. Pat's mum disappears towards the staff cloakroom. Pat waits. He turns towards Majid, smiles, and gives him a wink. He's right at the other end of the canteen, and Majid doesn't actually see the wink, but he knows that's what it was.

Pat's mum comes back, puts something in her son's hand, and warns him one last time. Pat takes it and thanks her. He tries to give her a kiss, but she won't let him. He tries again, just for the laugh.

She moves off with her trolley and doesn't look back.

'How much did she give you?' asks Majid.

'Hundred francs.'

'Good. You can get some cigarettes.

They head towards the station. Pat goes into the first tobacconist he sees. Majid waits outside. When his friend comes out with the cigarettes, he asks:

'What say we work the subway?'

'Exactly what I was thinking!'

They run to catch the train into Paris. Arriving at Saint-Lazare, they stay on the train until the ticket collectors disappear, then they make their way down to the Metro. They ignore the 'no entry' signs at the station exit and fight their way through the crowds coming up from the platform. They have a hard time carving a way through. Jostling on all sides. Modern times!

Pat is laughing to himself.

'I suppose you think this is funny,' says Majid in a tone of exasperation as he hangs on to the handrail.

'No – I was just thinking about what I told my mum.'

'What.'

'I told her I'd filled in an application form at the job centre. Ha, ha. . .! I'm some liar!'

'You don't really think she believed you, do you?'

'How should I know?'

'How can she have believed you – you can't even write!'

'Don't talk rubbish,' says Pat, threateningly. He doesn't like jokes about his school record.

Majid remembers the three years that Pat spent in the remedial class at school. He'd spent a year there himself.

The school authorities had set up a special section for children who were wholly or partially illiterate. They called it the remedial class. But it soon became known as the nutters' class. The other kids would point them out and make monkey faces at them.

This was where the teachers used to put all the riff-raff of the neighbourhood, all the future jail-birds. Balou and Pat held the all-time record – they rotted there for three long years. Even Raffin, the teacher of this weird class, wouldn't touch this pair with a barge pole, and he'd seen some rough ones in his time – gypsies, immigrants, the children of alcoholics and prostitutes and a variety of mental cases. And Raffin didn't do things by halves when it came to cramming the curriculum into their heads. Raffin ruled by the ruler – a whack across the head with a little box-wood number. But there's an exception to every rule, and Balou and Pat carried on measuring their cocks under the desk and spitting on their classmates.

Whenever a pupil looked like he couldn't keep up, and started holding back the rest of the class, the headmaster would send for Raffin. He'd arrive like an undertaker sizing up a corpse for burial. He'd grab the lad by the ear and eye him up and down, saying, 'The little ones, I break; the big ones, I squeeze!' The lad would lower his eyes, and Raffin would haul him off to his classroom. He'd sit him in the front desk, facing him, and he'd give him a mean look, followed by an evil smile that spoke volumes about what lay ahead for the boy.

Raffin got landed with all sorts – thieves, chatterboxes, brawlers, cheats, peeping Toms, lunatics and layabouts. He was proud of his ability to break them. But Balou and Pat proved too much for him – they reduced him to a state of quivering rage. Red in the face, like a bomb about to explode, and itching to beat the living daylights out of them. Even Raffin's breath – a mixture of garlic and cheap wine – didn't shake them. They enjoyed life in the remedial class, so what was the point of trying? They were the laughing-stock of the school, but who cared. . .!

There was nothing like threatening a pupil with Raffin to put the wind up him. It was worse than threatening him with the headmaster. Majid had spent a whole year in that class. It was just after his dad's accident, when he'd realized that the fall had left his father more or less like a vegetable, unable to control his children. The law of gravity came into operation, and he ended up somehow stuck to that desk.

It was winter when they put him in the remedial class. The grey suburban snows were already covering the estate, the same snow that had caused his father to fall from the roof where he was working.

Raffin was ill. Even with his long woollen scarf round his neck he was already coughing. He and Majid barely had time to make each other's acquaintance, because Raffin's coughing was getting worse by the day, and he could no longer carry on as he used to. When he shouted at them, it no longer had the same impact. He was getting weaker. There were rumours that he wouldn't last out the winter.

Even when Balou translated Archimedes' theorem into Archi Ahmed's Tea Room and had everyone in stitches, Raffin didn't throw the blackboard rubber at him. He didn't even react. Raffin was slipping. He no longer even sneaked off behind the boys' backs during lesson time to take a swig at the bottle of wine that he kept in a cupboard. The tamer of wild beasts had spent his health playing cat and mouse with these boys. The trouble was that the beasts they brought him were a fresh lot every year. The class never got older or grew up. The animals stopped roaring. It was if Raffin had broken down, and this had somehow unnerved them. They didn't provoke him any more, because he simply didn't react. He had become gentle, almost mild. They couldn't bring themselves to finish him off.

One afternoon, Raffin had a fresh bout of coughing. He didn't have time to get to the toilets. Or the strength. He vomited on the rostrum, down on his knees, hidden behind his desk. His pupils heard him choking and spluttering. A heavy, funereal silence filled the classroom. It was Pat and Balou, the old hands, who broke it.

Poor Raffin knelt there, his tongue hanging out, his eyes rolling, saliva dribbling into his legendary grey coat and snot hanging down his chin. He was still alive and breathing, but was wheezing badly. This last afternoon spent with Raffin left its mark on more than one boy in the class. Someone called the headmaster, who then called the police and an ambulance.

Who would ever have expected that the cops would come for Raffin! Usually the cops were there to bring back his students when they went missing.

Pat and Majid finally reach the platform, and they find a bench to sit on. They sit there for a while, waiting and watching for a promising handbag or a wallet sticking out of someone's pocket. From their point of view it's just one way among others of making a bit of money, and it's not their first time either.

In their slang 'working the Metro' means going pickpocketing. After all, when you're unemployed and getting no dole, you're not too fussy about how you get the price of a sandwich or a pack of cigarettes.

All of a sudden, a train pulls in and a large, thick-set man of about forty gets out. He's carrying a huge suitcase in his right hand. He's sweating. There's a woman with him, evidently his wife, and she's carrying an overnight bag. The man stands for a moment and pulls out a handkerchief to mop his brow. His wife waits for him. He's wearing a waist-length casual jacket which reveals a wallet sticking out of the back pocket of his trousers. Pat sees it, and nudges Majid to show him, since Majid is more likely to be watching the girls go by.

The woman and her sweating husband head off down the subway to change lines. Majid and Pat follow them. The man is obviously labouring under the weight of the suitcase, because he keeps changing hands. His wife shows her concern by mopping his brow with a handkerchief. Pat and Majid keep their distance, marking time when they need to, pretending to read the billboards. The fat man and his wife head for the platform marked 'Mairie d'Issy', and move to the middle of the platform where the first-class carriages stop.

The man puts his suitcase down and sighs. He pulls his handkerchief out and mops his brow again. He looks at his watch and says something to his wife. She nods in agreement. Pat walks up, on his own, and sits on a bench on the platform just behind them.

As the fat man stoops to put his suitcase down, his wallet works its way up a bit so that it sticks out even further. Majid walks up, casually, with his hands in his jacket pockets, and stands reading an advert a couple of yards up the platform. A number of other travellers are also waiting.

It's just coming up for two in the afternoon – the slack period.

The train comes round the bend. Majid walks up behind the fat man, taking care to be unobtrusive. The traveller picks up his case and steps forward towards the edge of the platform. Then Pat gets up, and pulls the zip of his bomber-jacket halfway down.

The train stops and a few passengers get off. The fat man gets on, followed by his wife. He picks up his heavy case with both hands so as to slide it in. Majid follows him on and jostles him heavily as he bends over to see to his baggage; at the same time he swiftly snatches the man's wallet with his left hand and turns to face the door.

There's a girl standing between Pat and Majid, a sweet little thing, just the way Pat likes them. She's smoothing her long hair with one hand as she admires herself in the glass door. Majid discreetly passes the wallet to Pat on his left. Pat moves off down the train, nonchalantly, as if absorbed in the subway map above the door.

Majid stays where he is, with his back turned to the couple. The doors close and the train picks up speed. The fat man and his wife are discussing which route to take. They talk quietly. Once again the man mops his face.

Majid watches the couple's reflection in the glass. The man tucks the damp handkerchief into his trouser pocket. Suddenly he reaches round to his back pocket.

He looks at his wife with an air of panic.

'My wallet's gone!'

'Are you sure?'

'Yes. Take a look in your handbag.'

The woman looks in her handbag and finds nothing. She says:

'Are you sure you didn't leave it at home?'

'I'm sure I had it. . . in fact, I put the tickets in it.'

He looks down at the floor just in case he's dropped it. . . and then he sees Majid.

He looks him up and down without a hint of embarrassment: an Arab!

He grabs the Arab by the collar and hauls him over:

'My wallet, you little shit!'

Majid shrinks away as if scared of the man. Half trembling, he protests.

'Leave me alone! I haven't done anything!'

Then he shouts:

'This man's insane! He's off his head!'

He sees Pat laughing to himself down the carriage. He continues shouting:

'What gives you the right. . . eh? I've got nothing to do with your wallet. It's always like this – they see an Arab, and straight away he's a thief!'

The fat man flattens him against the door and Majid allows himself to be searched, protesting all the while. The man gives him a thorough going-over – front, back, crutch and all.

'Do you want me to take my shoes off as well?' asks Majid. 'And my underpants too?'

The fat man feels he's made a fool of himself. He's almost apologetic. Some of the passengers shrink back at the sight of an Arab walking their way.

Majid turns to the man.

'So what now?'

The train pulls into the next station, and a number of people get off. Majid gets off too, glaring at the couple all the while. Pat's got off by another door and is heading for the exit. The fat man is upset, and says a few words to his wife. Majid plays his part to the full, and hurls a final insult in their direction before turning to follow Pat.

Pat's waiting for him at the top of the steps, grinning. They're at Madeleine station. Pat pulls the wallet out of his jacket and searches it, having first checked that there are no police about. The princely sum of two one-hundred-franc notes!

'Some killing! We won't get far on that!'

They head off down to Strasbourg-Saint-Denis.

They call in for a bite at a snackbar on Faubourg Saint-Martin. A chili sausage in a roll for Majid and a ham roll for Pat, followed by a beer each. Then they stroll along Boulevard Sébastopol to Châtelet. They take a turn round rue Saint-Denis, to check out the prostitutes. Pat even goes over and asks one of them – all done up like a TV dancer – what she charges, but she is too expensive for him. He tries haggling over the price, and then points to Majid:

'My pal's got a family discount card. Does he get a reduction?'

To which the girl replies:

'Why don't you just piss off and leave me alone?'

'Bitch,' says Pat, as he walks on.

The girl doesn't answer. Just scowls at them. When they find a good-looking girl, preferably not wearing a lot, they go over to check her out. . . 'I fancy a screw,' says Pat. 'I've got a hell of a hard-on!'

'We can go back. We'll go see Josephine.'

'OK — before her man gets back from work.'

They catch the subway again, and then the overground train, back to where they live.

Pat wastes no time – he goes straight up to Josephine's.

Majid doesn't go with him. He decides he'd rather go home.

'See you later,' says Pat.

'Yeah,' says Majid.

The lift's jammed somewhere, so Majid has to take the service stairs. He carefully avoids the puddles of piss.

On the third floor he finds Farid sitting on a step. Farid lifts his head, recognizes him, and gives him a feeble smile.

'What's up? What are you doing here?

Farid doesn't reply. With his hands crossed on his knees he stares straight in front of him.

'Hey, hey!' Majid shakes him. Farid doesn't budge.

'Things not going too well, eh, Rusty?'

Still no answer. So Majid lifts him up to take him home.

Pat rings at Josephine's front door. She opens, but doesn't want to let him in.

'No, Patrick – my husband will be back soon.'

'Don't be silly,' says Pat. 'It's only four-thirty.'

Josephine is pretty. Her long, chestnut hair, done up in a bun, highlights her big hazel eyes. She's wearing a sleeveless dress that shows nicely rounded shoulders.

She's holding a baby to her breast, an eight-month-old that she tries to comfort at the same time as trying to shut the door on Pat.

He doesn't want to go, though. He forces his way in.

Josephine's other child, a three-year-old girl, comes up and tugs at her dress, saying repeatedly: 'Mummy, mummy. . .'

Pat shuts the door and kisses Josephine on the neck.

Josephine struggles: 'Patrick, don't be stupid. . .' But Pat carries on being stupid. Taking advantage of the fact that Josephine's got the kid in her arms, he kisses her on the mouth.

Josphine shrinks back.

'Not in front of the little ones, for God's sake!'

Pat lets go of her. She sees to her daughter, who's still holding her by the dress, and goes down the hallway to one of the bedrooms. Pat goes into the living-room and kicks off his shoes. He hears Josephine comforting the children. He takes off his jeans, and Josephine reappears without the kids.

'You could have come earlier. . .!'

As he folds his jeans, Pat replies, 'I couldn't make it, earlier.'

She takes off her light dress to reveal two firm, white, chubby breasts that smell of baby.

As she takes her knickers off, Pat is already flat out on the couch ready to take her. She positions herself on top of him, parting her thighs to settle herself on his sex.

'What about Majid?' she asks.

He doesn't answer, preferring to press his lips against hers. He lets her hair down, and her long chestnut locks fall like freshly-scythed corn, hiding his face.

Majid takes Farid home. At the front door he tells him:
    'Stand up straight.'
    Farid tries. His pasty complexion, his raggedy hair, with one lock falling over his eyes, gives him a mean look – no mistaking, the face of an addict.
    The door is opened by Farid's big brother. He's built like a brick shithouse. When he sees Farid, his torso swells angrily under his Italian vest.
    'Where did you find this bastard?' he asks Majid.
    'On the staircase.'
    Abdallah grabs his younger brother by the collar and hurls him down the corridor. Farid crashes to the floor in the living-room. Majid didn't expect this. All he can do is shout:
    'Gently – you'll hurt him!'
    'What the fuck's that to do with you?' the brother yells, ready to lash out a second time.
    Majid goes to help Farid, who's still half-stoned, and takes him to his room.
    'A bunch of wankers, that's all you are,' the big brother continues. 'You think you're so clever, getting stoned out of your minds and behaving like arseholes. Look at the state of him, look at him. . . He's fucked. . .'
    In the living-room, a little old Arab woman in an oriental dress is sitting cross-legged on a carpet. Her head is covered by a turban and she is praying. Her hands are counting off the pearl beads of a Muslim rosary, as if she is oblivious to what's happening in the corridor.

The shouting continues. With difficulty, Farid lies down on his bed and hides his face in his hands. They can hear Abdallah, nervous as a tiger, still ranting and swearing in the room next door – his sister Naima's room.

She's only sixteen, a pretty kid, and pregnant already. A disgrace to her family. . . Everyone on the estate knows she's pregnant. Rumours spread fast here. That's why Abdallah doesn't let her go out any more. You have to hide you family misfortunes.

She could have had an abortion, if she hadn't been so scared of telling her family. She would have got a good hiding from her brother, but that would have been that. There are plenty of abortions on this estate. The girls have no idea about contraception, and the men couldn't care less, as long as they get a screw.

'Who's going to marry you now?' her mother would grumble. 'Eh? Tell me! How are you going to find a husband with a baby on your hands, eh? Dirty little bitch. . .!'

Majid thinks of all this as he stands in the hallway. As he passes the door, he can see Naima sitting on her bed holding her belly. She no longer combs her hair, she looks pale, and her face is thin and haggard. With all the insults, all the kickings that she's had to endure, she has no tears left to cry.

In the evening, the grandmother brings her a bowl of soup and a bit of bread. She eats it in her room.

As for her father, he'd come within an ace of killing her, one night when he'd come home drunk. He wanted to throw her from the window. She screamed, and her cries echoed round the estate. Fortunately, her mother stepped in to stop him. And from that moment they took care to keep her out of sight of her father, particularly when he was drunk.

Majid goes home. His mum's not in, because it's the end of the working-day and she's out cleaning offices. In the living-room, his younger brother Mehdi is doing his homework. With his head in his hands and his elbows on a little table that Majid rescued from the basement, the kid's struggling over a maths textbook.

Majid never did much homework when he was at school. As soon as classes were over, he'd chuck his schoolbag into a ditch, and out would come the football. They'd organize their matches on the nearest waste ground, games that never ended, with twenty or more players, and with their schoolbags as goal posts. The kids got into it like animals after a day of enforced captivity. You needed to know how to dribble if you wanted to caress that ball, with all the yearnings and the passionate limbs that surrounded it. And in order to make a pass, you had to take the ball with love and a delicate touch. With all these guys between you and your partner, you'd have to throw some wicked dummies.

That's where the world's great soccer players come from. A swerve of the body, total control of the ball, is not learnt just to show off, but so as to keep the ball from everybody else. The same goes for the art of dribbling: those outstanding players who bring crowds to their feet all learnt their art on pieces of wasteland, in the survival of the fittest and the most selfish.

Lessons and homework took second place.

At the time, Majid and his parents were living in the Nanterre bidonville — the rue de la Folie — the largest and the cruellest of any in the Paris suburbs. Shantytowns that could equal anything in Brazil, but without the sun and the music. When Majid's dad had sent for his wife and son to come from Algeria, he'd not told them in his letter that they'd be coming to live in a cold, smoky barracks. When she first saw the place, Malika burst into tears, and Majid wondered if it was some kind of practical joke, because back home there was never enough to eat, but at least you had your little stone-built house; at least you had a home. You can always hide an empty stomach, but a hovel is there for all to see. Whatever happened to dignity? Malika used to clutch her little boy in her arms and wish she'd never made the voyage. His father used to say:

'They're going to rehouse us somewhere decent. . . I've been down to see them at the Town Hall. . .'

Months, years, spent living on their nerves – and always on the alert for fires, because in the shanty town the fires were a weekly event. Some-times they were huge and lasted for hours. People would finally go back to bed in the early hours of the morning, with the flames dying down and the firemen exhausted.

Majid was seven years old when he and his mother found themselves waiting, one November morning, on the platform of a Paris station. His father was supposed to be meeting them, but he wasn't there. They waited for him, wandering around the station as the early editions hit the news stands and commuters stood drinking their morning coffees. Malika was still wearing her veil – as if caught between two civilizations. The suburban commuters on their way to clock in at the office eyed her curiously. This was the first time she'd left her village in Eastern Algeria, and here she was, all of a sudden, catapulted to the other side of the Mediterranean. Everything seemed so very huge here. 'This must be progress,' she told herself behind her veil. She had bought a new *haik* specially for the trip. It was her best outfit, and she wore it only to discover that women don't wear them here. Finally Majid's dad arrived, dressed in his fez. Majid didn't recognize him – when his father had emigrated, he had been too young to know him. He let himself be kissed by the man, because Malika told him that this was his father.

Then came the taxi, and then the shanty town. Young Majid went out looking for kids, and there were kids everywhere. 'Don't go getting lost,' Malika would tell him when he went out.

He was surprised by the Arab children – they all spoke French! And the kids weren't worried by this

slum city, with its mud and its piles of rotting garbage. They spent their time – the Arab kids, with
the Portuguese and the French — playing among the
wrecked cars.

The football pitch is a sight to see. It's next to the
street, and the goalposts are four big oil drums filled
with stones. It's cold here. Majid's cheeks are blue
and his lips are trembling, but nobody pays any
attention to him. He wanders round the village.
It's a real labyrinth, but it's organized. It's got a
butcher's, a grocer's, a café-bar, a restaurant, and
even a hairdresser's. A letterbox at the side of
the road serves as a target for the kids' catapults.
The one who gets his stone through the slot is the
winner.

  The children seem happy enough as they play in
among the mud and the poverty and the thick smoke
from people's stoves. Kids always seem to make
out somehow – they'd find themselves somewhere
to play even in a minefield. . .!

  Majid enrols at the local school. His pals from the
shanty town are easily recognizable by the mud on
their shoes. It's not even worth cleaning shoes like
that. You'd have to be an acrobat to avoid the mud
– there was a long trek between the shantytown and
the main road, and you could hardly do it on your
head!

  God, that playground is huge on your first day
at school when you don't know anyone! It's like a
football game – you have to mark out the opposition
if you don't want to end up screwed. Majid is one of
those with a will to fight. A survivor. He can never

sit at the back as part of a herd – he has to be in front, at the top, all the time, even if it is exhausting, because it's not a lot of fun out there on your own. If you don't want to be on your own, then you have to take others along with you – but they're usually such losers that you're better off going it alone.

That evening, when Majid returns home, he finds his mother sitting at the kitchen table peeling potatoes. Malika's sitting on a chair, but Majid hasn't got used to chairs yet. In Algeria, everyone used to sit on the floor to eat and talk. But not here, because what will the neighbours think. . .?

His mum is deeply unhappy. She can't keep the walls clean, because they're made of board. Can't clean the floor either – no point in using a floor-cloth because it's a dirt floor, and if you sweep it, all you get is clouds of dust. She doesn't even dare go out, because women don't wear veils here, and she's scared to go out without her *haik*. She still can't find the courage to do it, so it's left to Majid to go and fetch the water from the communal tap. There's just one tap for the whole shanty town. In winter it freezes solid and has to be thawed out. The inhabitants bring newspaper, strips of wood, cardboard boxes and crates, and they build a fire round it. And while they wait they sit on jerry-cans, making the most of the warmth and talking of this and that.

Every now and then someone fiddles with the tap to see if any water's coming through. To get it to run, you have to heat it up, say a prayer, and wait for a miracle. You might as well call in a witch doctor or do a rain dance round it, for all the good it does.

All this provides an entertaining spectacle for the residents of the surrounding tower-blocks. They're all right – they've got hot water on tap. You can see them looking out at you. There's probably one of Majid's classmates up there somewhere, watching him. . . well fed, freshly bathed and warmly dressed in clean pyjamas and slippers. He doesn't like to look up; he turns back to the fire.

The tap remains frozen for most of the winter and has to be thawed out two or three times a day. As for the toilets, they're just a big hole with two planks over it, inside a hut that has no roof.

It took Malika a long time to get used to all this. Sometimes, though, on a Sunday afternoon, they'd invite their relations round for a meal in their shack. Then she was happy, because the conversation turned to life in the old country. When friends criticized her for not going out, she'd just shrug her shoulders. What's the point? It's so cold in this country. . . the sky is always so grey. . . Majid used to do his homework sitting on his bed, next to a little coal stove, using a chair for a desk.

Then, after the bare boards of the shantytown, came the concrete. . .

Majid stretches out on his bed and watches his younger brother tidying his schoolbooks away.

A string of images races through his head. He prefers to let them pass. He has no desire to go searching among his memories. He is tired.

The little one closes his satchel and leaves the room. Majid gets up and stretches. Malika will be home from work soon, so he'd best leave, because she's bound to be in a bad mood, and he'll end up in trouble. He decides he'd best go to Pat's.

The door is opened by Chantal, Pat's big sister.

'Hi.'

Chantal calls to her big brother.

'It's Majid.'

Pat emerges from the kitchen, biting into a green apple.

'You see your sister?' Majid jokes. 'I mean to say, ever since she's been working, she won't give me a kiss. Swanking about. . . if you ask me, she's getting too big for her boots. . .'

'You'd best shut up,' Pat advised, 'otherwise there'll be another row.'

'She's still got a lovely arse, though.'

And Chantal shouts from the kitchen:

'Shut up, you tosser!'

'You hear that?' Majid observes. 'I mean to say. . .!'

'Don't push your luck,' Pat warns. Majid continues in the same teasing vein:

'Chantal!'

'Yeah?'

'I tell you, if I had a pretty little arse like yours, I wouldn't waste my time working in an office.'

Chantal comes into the room, hands on hips, and gives Majid a look that says she's not amused: 'Piss off – you're getting on my nerves.'

Majid scratches his head:

'OK, keep your hair on. . . I tell you, Pat, I don't know what's got into young people these days. . . Can't take a joke any more, not like the old days. . .'

Pat puts on his jacket and pulls on his boots. In the doorway Majid stops for a moment and eyes her up again:

'God, look at that arse! And those tits!!'

When they get to Maggy's, all the gang is there. Anita is on the pinball machine. She's a one-woman noise machine in her own right as she bangs hell out of the flippers. Thierry, Bengston, Jean-Marc and Bibiche are all on the table-football. Pat and Majid decide to go and tease Anita. They lean their elbows on the glass top of the pinball machine, and start discussing the weather.

'Piss off,' says Anita. 'Don't muck about. . . I can't see the ball. . . I'm going to lose it.'

She hops about like a flea. Pat gropes her, while Majid blows cigarette smoke in her eyes.

'Stop it, will you?!'

Then she gets fed up, gives the table a jolt and sends it into tilt.

'Now look what you've made me do!'

Pat goes over to her, lips pouting.

'I love you, Anita. . . Give us a kiss, babe!'

She recoils from him.

'I'm crazy for you, doll.' Anita does not think this is funny. She escapes to Maggy over at the cash desk.

Majid laughs and goes to watch the table-football.

Pat grabs Anita by the waist and pulls her to him. She puts up a struggle.

'Leave her alone, you!' says Maggy. 'Or I'll throw you out.'

Pat lets go.

'Even the grown-ups can't take a joke any more. . . What's the world coming to?' he sighs. And he raises his hands in despair.

The door opens. It's Solange, with her little boy in her wake. She shuts the door behind her and stands in the entrance, her mouth drawn and tense, as she watches the scene from behind a haze of alcohol.

'The first person to move buys me a drink!'

Nobody moves. They all ignore her.

'What a bunch of. . . Not one of them lifts a finger. . .!'

She goes to the bar and orders a beer, while her son heads for the table-football. Maggy refuses to serve her and tells her that she's had enough.

Solange complains to the world at large:

'What's the matter? My money not good enough?'

Still they ignore her. When Maggy says no, there's no point in arguing. . .

'I haven't robbed your till, have I? I haven't got the pox, have I. . .? So. . .?'

Maggy deals with her gently, almost like a mother:

'You've had enough to drink for today, eh? You just go home to your mother-in-law and put the little one to bed. Look at him. He's dead on his feet, poor thing!'

The sentimental approach usually works with Solange. She looks at her kid. He's not as sleepy as Maggy claims, though. . . He's still got his drink, and he's totally absorbed in the table-football.

Christmas was on its way. Malika took her children – the three youngest – to the town hall, to get their Christmas presents. Every year, the local council gives away free shoes to children in need.

They went to catch the bus. It was cold outside.

Malika was already in a bad mood when she got up that morning – tired even before the day had started.

She had got to bed very late the night before. Levesque had been at it again. All but strangled his wife — she still had the marks on her neck. As Eric and Fabienne were asleep, they'd not heard their parents fighting. Levesque's wife had bitten his hand; then she'd started screaming. This woke Eric, and he ran to get Malika, who fortunately was not asleep yet. She came in to find Levesque running around stark naked, and his wife too.

'She bit me, the bitch. I'll teach you to show some respect for your husband,' he yelled, as he ducked round Malika, trying to get his hands on his wife. She must have refused to do him a complete blow-job. But how could anyone do a blow-job for a person as egotistical, as repulsive, as low-life as this arsehole husband of hers? How could anyone love an evil-minded, drunken wreck like this?

Malika could imagine the scene: Levesque would have demanded his favourite treat; she must have refused at first, but then accepted because she was scared of him; she'd sucked him off, but refused to let him come in her mouth. Levesque would have taken her by the throat, half throttled her, and she, with luck, would have sunk her teeth into his cock!

Levesque took a long time calming down, and the bastard still wasn't asleep!

His wife had grabbed the kids and taken refuge at Malika's. They'd made a cup of tea while they waited for the beast to stop roaring in his cage. When Majid finally returned at about two in the morning, Malika had sent him to see if 'm'sieu Livisque' had cooled off yet. Yes, he was asleep, so his family were able to return home. But the fear was still there, and so was the despair. . .

The shoes that they were giving away were great big winter shoes, the kind that kick you on the shins in the playground and leave you with a bruise. . . The town hall was swarming with people.

In the huge hall on the ground floor, mothers were watching their kids trying on the shoes, making sure they got the right size. Neighbours met each other and paused for a chat. It gave Malika pleasure to be able to show off her kids – well turned out, good-mannered, and spotlessly clean. The kids were all happy with their shoes, except for Ounissa, the youngest girl, who complained that she didn't want that sort because they were boys' shoes. Malika

took them anyway – but took a size bigger, to fit
Stephane.

'Chousette' still hasn't found a job. Sometimes
she gets desperate. Her husband's not giving her
money for the housekeeping any more. She's been to
report him to the Welfare, but he's gone off without
leaving a forwarding address, and now she's got
Christmas and the New Year facing her. It's going
to be hell.

Finally she decides to take her little one to her
parents for Christmas, near Orleans. She knows
that her mother will keep on at her about her
marriage. She can hear it already: 'Don't say we
didn't warn you. . . But you had to do it your way,
didn't you. . .'

She's not sure that she'll be able to face it.

On New Year's Day, her sister Kathy will be
there – happily married, two kids, a car, a husband in a good job, just around the corner from
her mum's, everything going for her. Josette feels
the noose tightening; she feels overwhelmed by the
hopelessness and pointlessness of it all. The silence
is beginning to grate on her nerves. At times like
Christmas, you can't help imagining that everybody
else is having a good time, especially when you see
them all leaping about on TV. . .

Stephane stares wide-eyed at the little Christmas
tree and his tiny presents. Josette's had to scrimp
and save to buy them. She has to make out that
everything's OK. At midnight, she gives her kiddy
a big kiss, just like they're all doing on TV. But also
because she needs it; she has a huge need for a bit of
human warmth, a place of refuge, a last ray of hope.

On Saturdays the estate brightens up a bit. The population seems somehow more real. They've all had a lie-in, and down they come, looking relaxed and pulling their shopping trolleys behind them. Off to the market, or the shops, or the supermarket. And there's Malard, his fat little body wedged into a tight-fitting track-suit, taking his alsatian for a walk. He's teaching it to piss in the gutter.

'Sit. . . Stay. . . Walk. . .' he orders.

And the dog obeys. Malard is delighted. He flexes his muscles, watches the passers-by, and starts again.

The sun illuminates the concrete briefly, as it shines on the top of the central tower-block. Out on the balconies and in people's windows it's time for the dance of the broom – the big weekly sweep-out. Doormats, carpets, rugs, all shaken into the wind, vomiting their load of dust onto the neighbours below.

A naked Coquelouche – the one whose wife ran off with Pat's dad – stands at his window scanning the scantily-dressed housewives on the surrounding balconies with a pair of binoculars. By the end of its fifth return trip, the lift gives up the ghost. Curses and insults echo up and down the stair-well, but then people go out of their way to be polite to each other, to say good morning and to make way for each other. This usually involves stepping in a puddle of piss, and they apologize to each other as they drag their shopping trolleys along, with a resigned smile that seems to say: 'Oh well. . . It's not the end of the world. . .'

Most people drive to go to the supermarket, even though it's only just down the road. Ten minutes on foot, but it's an excuse to use the car, which hasn't moved all week. The only time it sees any action is on Saturday mornings, for the shopping, and Sunday afternoons, when they go to visit the in-laws.

The real joke is when August comes around: three-quarters of the population set off in their cars and head for the sun, in search of a tan, leaving a bit of space for the others to breathe. When they go to the country, they take everything – the fridge, the TV, the washing machine – even the dog, if they haven't managed to dump it in a field somewhere. Whether they're caravanning or camping, they'd take the tower-block with them if they could. They have a celebratory drink when they set off, and a celebratory drink when they leave to come back again, so they're drunk both ways, coming and going. Some of them never come back at all, because Mr Monte-Carlo Rally falls asleep at the wheel. Some of them come back with one member of the crew missing, because he swam out too far and got washed away. They rush to send off their postcards, with pictures of thousands of people just like themselves lying in

rows on the beach, and words to the effect of: 'The
food's nice here, and the weather's good.' Dad gets
sunburn on his head, mum comes up in blisters and
the kids come out in spots. They vow to go somewhere else next year.

The kids from the concrete jungle head straight
for the Côte d'Azur. If you're going to steal wallets,
you might as well make it worth your while. The
word is that you get big wallets round Saint-Tropez,
crocodile, lizard-skin, that sort of thing, and even
if there's nothing in them, you can always sell the
wallets.

What's more, you get nice tits on the Côte. Check-
out girls from the Paris supermarkets (where they
sell despair in packets of six for the price of one),
who fancy themselves as starlets and pretend to
come from high-class homes, are more of a turn-
on than farm-girls in Brittany. So when you're not
thieving, you can sit and watch the girls.

You get yourself a John Travolta haircut, you
steal yourself a pair of swimming trunks from the
market, and a tube of sun-tan lotion of course,
and you stretch out on the beach. You lie in wait
for designer handbags, most particularly the ones
that sit there all alone because mademoiselle has
gone for a dip. Then there are the ones that come
back straight away, pronto pronto, because they've
got the boys in blue on their tails, and the others
who don't get back till six months or a year later
– because the law ran faster than they did!

Like all the immigrants, Malika prefers the market
at Gennevilliers, where there are three long rows

of exclusively Arab stalls. It feels like being back home.

There's a smell of fresh mint, wild mint, still damp with the dew. In Algeria, you'd often see people out strolling, holding a sprig of mint to their noses, enjoying its refreshing smell. There's *rassoul*, there's real *khol*, there's *souak* – the bark of the sweet chestnut tree, which the women chew after bathing so as to whiten their teeth and give their gums a henna tinge. There's also *chiba*, the small green-grey plant that people infuse in their tea. In the Gennevilliers market you find all the herbs and spices of the North African coastline.

In the days before her husband fell on his head, Malika used to buy a live chicken every Saturday. She'd carry it around in her shopping basket, with its head sticking out. Since she wasn't the only one with a live chicken, the racket on the bus was unbelievable. Not to mention all the relations having high-volume conversations the length and breadth of the bus. The local white population didn't particularly appreciate this, which is probably why they usually went to market by car.

'Hamdulillah!' 'Hamdulillah!'

And so saying, they'd stuff the chicken's head back into the basket, to stop it squawking.

Now that the old man's sick, he's no longer able to cut the chickens' throats, so Malika doesn't buy chicken any more. Or she has to go to her next-door neighbour, who knows the right way to do it.

This involves saying a little prayer before the creature goes to meet its maker. Then you pull its tongue out to the right, turn its head to face Mecca, say another prayer, and wham! You cut the chicken's throat so that it bleeds and then keep it in the bath to stop it running all round the flat.

In the bidonvilles, they used to kill the chickens outdoors, and then they'd let them run. The birds would take their last run up alleyways, chased by a crowd of kids, until they finally fell over in the mud.

On Saturdays, Levesque's already drunk by midday. When he's done his shopping, he goes round the bars, basket in hand. There he finds Mimile, Dédé, Nénesse, Jacquot and all the gang, and they each set up a round of pastis. A bet on the horses and it's time for another round.

'One more, to forget. . .'

'In that case you'd better pay straight away!'

And the arseholes fall about laughing.

They corner the local carpet-seller – the one with the face of a tourist-brochure Arab. He smiles all the time. He understands the Frenchmen's racist jibes, but he still smiles. Every time he sells one of his carpets, that's his revenge, because every time they buy one, they've been swindled.

'Who needs oil when you've got Ricard?!'

'That's not allowed by Allah!'

'Your health!'

Mimile's very tickled with his joke. He slaps his thighs.

The kids come out of school and make their way noisily across the estate. No school dinners on Saturday – they eat at home. No school in the afternoon either, so they're happy. Now that they're on a forty-hour week like their proletarian parents, with homework and extra classes thrown in, they have no time to come out and play – not unless they can grab a bit of time back from parents and teachers. These kids have had enough of being kept under lock and key. They're the ones who stare out of the classroom window while the others have their eyes on the blackboard. Out in the street, they play hide-and-seek behind the parked cars, or bang each other over the head with their schoolbooks.

Malika returns with three large loaves under her left arm and a shopping bag full of fruit, meat and vegetables on her right. Her husband follows her. He's good for just about nothing these days, but he can still follow her and carry her shopping bag. Next to Malika, he looks tiny. He doesn't pull his weight any more.

The kids are already back. They're nibbling dry bread and the left-overs of small cakes. They take a drink of water, drinking straight from the tap. As soon as the shopping has been put away, Malika makes her ablutions, to prepare herself for prayer. She shuts herself in the bathroom and washes the full length of her arms and then her calves. She washes her face once, rinses round her teeth, passes her hand over her face again, and murmurs, 'Allah akbar.' Then she goes to her bedroom and prays, kneeling on a goatskin that's been brought over from Algeria, and facing in the supposed direction of Mecca. She does this four times a day. She talks to her god with her eyes half closed and her hands together in prayer. She prays for Majid, for Josette, for a better life for the poor and the underprivileged. She prays for strength and protection. 'Allah akbar.'

Then she gets up slowly and goes to face the world of humans.

The humans are all sitting round the table, hungry. They're waiting for the cucumber salad that Amaria's preparing. They're getting impatient. They play with the cutlery. Malika has taken out a dozen eggs for her famous Saturday afternoon garlic and tomato omelette. The only one who is relaxed is the father. They sit him on a chair at the table, and switch on the TV. He sits there and doesn't budge. It's as if he's the baby of the family. He's quite happy to sit there and watch the flickering screen. Sometimes little Ounissa comes and sits on his knee and cuddles up to him. He smiles awkwardly and rests his daughter's cheek on his head. It's impossible to say what's going through his mind, but at least he must feel that this flat is home. He's a bit like a dog — he recognizes his owners, but if you dumped him in the middle of a field, he'd be in trouble. He'd never starve, though; he'd just go with the first person to whistle to him. . .

For Pat and Majid, Saturday is a day like any other –
except for the evenings, when they get together with
their friends.

At the Alhambra, the midnight session is usually
a porno film. Every hooligan for miles around
makes it their rendezvous. The scene is indescrib-
able – an appalling racket of shouting, insults,
cheers and jeers. The usherette tries to get them to
shut up, but no chance – they call her every name
under the sun. The owner of the cinema keeps well
out of the way. He's been roughed up on too many
previous occasions. . . And in the auditorium, they
smoke, they spit, they hold conversations between
the balcony and the stalls. . . and they swap the
latest news:

'Hey – Maxie's been sent down!'

'Oh?'

'He did over a jeweller's. . .'

'He'll get a good stretch for that.'

'You know James – the one with the limp?'

'The blond kid with the spotty face?'

'That's the one. Well, he killed himself coming off
his bike on the Pontoise motorway. On the way to
see his girlfriend.'

'Too bad.'

Then all of them gather in the corner café. You usually find two rival gangs in there, scuffling at the bar. They've got nothing better to do, so they fight. Sometimes it turns really nasty, especially for the poor sod who ends up on the floor getting a kicking. One Bastille Day, the local neighbourhood dance was broken up by a mass brawl – the biggest the estate had ever seen – easily fifty of them, going at one another with bottles, knives and knuckle-dusters. The cops wouldn't even come near it. . .!

Maggy really liked the gang, and they felt the same about her. She used to call them her 'little ones'. In her bar you'd always find a bit of human warmth, a pal, a cigarette, or a couple of francs to tide you over. There was never any trouble at Maggy's either: if they wanted to fight, they did it off the premises. Her son Noel was inside for robbery. He was usually part of the gang. She didn't blame the gang, though. That particular evening, there was a raid by the police. The familiar routine: produce your wage packet, your ID papers, your dole card. . . Those who weren't students and who couldn't produce a wage slip – in other words the majority – got the 'treatment'. The cops took their ID cards and went to the car outside to radio the station, to check you out, to see if you were on the wanted list, see if you had a record. . .

One of the cops asked Pat for his papers. Pat refused. The cop was furious. He repeated his request:

'Your papers!'

Pat continued drinking his beer, casually, to show his pals that he wasn't afraid. He replied:

'I'm French. This is my country. What do you take me for, an Arab?'

'Mind who you're talking to.'

Pat put his glass on the bar and replied, cockily:

'So why do you want to see my papers, then?'

'There's going to be trouble if you refuse.'

Pat wasn't particularly keen on being taken for a spin in the paddy-wagon, so he pulled out a dirty, dog-eared ID card. The cop held it gingerly, as if he was afraid of getting infected. He asked Pat for his name and address, and then returned his card. They still dragged off two of the local lads, though, for looking shifty. What had they done? Nobody knew.

Once the cops had gone, Bibiche pulled out a couple of grammes of hash that he'd stashed in the goal of the table football machine. Maggy was furious.

Pat cursed the police as he heard their car start.

'Bastards.'

Majid paid for everyone's drinks before he left – which prompted Thierry to comment:

'You been fishing today, then?'

'I pay for your drinks, and you start asking questions?!'

'No need to get ratty; I was only joking.'

'Well don't.'

The four of them went out together – Majid, Pat, Bengston and Thierry. It was already dark, and there was a chill in the air. Just as they were arriving at the entrance to the estate, they saw a young Arab lad by name of Lousef — nicknamed Lulu. He was completely drunk, and was more or less unsuccessfully trying to piss against the

railings. He could hardly stand up. They were surprised at the state of him. As they came towards
him, he was pissing on his boots. They waited
behind him until he finally noticed there was someone there. Without even putting his cock back in his
fly he grabbed at the railings with both hands. He
was breathing heavily. Pat said:

'Lucky they put those railings there.'

The others smiled.

Lulu turned round with difficulty. He was still
more or less holding onto the railings with his left
hand. He looked at them, peered more closely, and
finally recognized them. 'Oh, it's you. . . bunch of
wankers. . .'

Bengston laughed, and said:

'Close your shop. You're showing your tools.'

'What?'

'Put your dick away, or someone might cut it
off.'

Lulu looked down and saw his cock hanging out.
He put it away. 'What you been up to, dum-dum?'
Majid asked.

Lulu tried to speak, but the effort just made him
throw up. The others laughed and dived out of the
way as he vomited all over the railings. He wiped
his mouth with his shirt-sleeve and confided:

'It's old Malard's wine. . . and. . . ha. . . ha. . .
it's good stuff!!'

He laughed along with the others. 'I got it from
his basement, the old bastard. . . Ha, ha. . .!'

The others took him by the arm and led him off.

'We're going to check if you're talking rubbish or
not.'

They walked round the parking-lot and went through the hallway of Poppy House. Thierry turned on the light in the basement corridor. He found Malard's cellar door wide open. Several empty bottles were lying on the floor. There were five whole crates of wine sitting there! Good stuff, too. They set to, drinking straight from the bottle. Lulu laughed as he watched them. 'Hmm. . . Not bad at all,' said Pat, with the air of a connoisseur.

They tucked two or three bottles apiece inside their jackets, and went to leave. Pat let out a burp in the empty corridor, followed by a sigh of relief. Thierry predicted:

'Nice one! We'll be well pissed by tonight. . .'

They went out by the back entrance and made their way through the dark to Azalea House, where Pat and Majid lived.

Here too they made for the basement. Lulu could hardly stand up, so Thierry had to more or less drag him. Majid said to the others: 'We'll go and see Rusty.'

They found Rusty in the basement, together with Miloud and Delphine, two other residents of Acacia House, in the process of smoking a joint. Bengston said:

'Hello, lads. We've brought the gargle.'

Delphine – the redhead – jumped at the sound of his voice. Miloud – the Moroccan – stuck out his hand for a bottle. Pat gave him one. They sat next to each other in the tiny cellar and opened their bottles. Thierry rolled another joint.

Bengston chuckled to himself.

'Can you imagine Malard's face when he sees his wine's gone?'

The others laughed, and Majid said that it served him right. Pat was sitting next to Delphine. He took her by the shoulder and kissed her on the cheek. Sitting there with her eyes closed and her legs crossed. Pat put his hand on her breast and kissed her on the mouth.

'Leave us a bit, will you,' Thierry asked, as he lit the joint.

Delphine leaned her head on Pat's shoulder and continued her trip. Each of them in turn took a gentle drag on the joint. With the help of the wine, they were soon flying high, and silence settled on the proceedings. The smoke of the joint rose vertically before flattening out against the ceiling. It filled the cellar with a heavy, bitter odour, and made them even more thirsty. Lulu fell asleep on Miloud's shoulder.

It was a moment of peace and contemplation. To hell with the unemployment, the concrete jungle, and the worries. Peace and quiet, and a bit of human warmth, like when you're falling asleep after an over-busy day. Time didn't matter any more – the only thing that mattered was the here and now. Yesterday was a washout, but tomorrow, who knows. . . Shit – someone's been dragging too hard on the joint; so it's tightened up. You'd bust your lungs trying to get a draw now. They put so much energy into it – energy that turns into boredom, the energy that they stockpile because it's impossible for them to do what they really want to do, to use it to some useful end.

There they were, at peace with the world and flying high, when suddenly a tear-gas canister exploded against the wall opposite the cellar door. Everyone in the cellar panicked. Wrenched out of their day-dreams, they scrambled for the exit. Delphine was screaming with fear. Pat held her by the hand and pulled her towards the exit. Thierry and Majid saw to Lousef, who was still pissed as a rat, and Farid, who was completely out of it and coughing badly.

They raced out of their hideaway to escape the blinding gas. From the basement they had to go up several stairs before they reached the fresh air of the hallway.

There they found the 'militia' waiting for them. The 'militia' was a group of tenants – many of them parents themselves – who were exasperated by the continual thefts, the vandalism, the stolen or burned-out cars. . . They had decided to play at cops themselves. In a group they felt strong – driven on by their hatred of the youth and by the fear that they whip up among themselves, and which is regularly fed by the media. When they go on a sortie, they arm themselves with billy-clubs and iron bars. On this particular evening, there were a dozen of them waiting at the top of the stairs for the young people who were now choking on the fumes of their gas.

Pat was the first to come up, followed by Delphine. He stopped dead when he saw Finet – Jean-Marc's dad – whose car he'd burned out the night before; Langlois was also there; Malard too, obviously; Yvon and his alsatian, and other assorted heavies, all wearing tracksuits and armed to the teeth. Thierry, Miloud, Bengston and Majid came up and stood next to Pat. They were still dazed.

'Come on, then, let's have you. . .' Finet called, as a challenge. 'I thought young people today were supposed to be fearless,' said Langlois, toying with his club.

Pat zipped up his jacket, ready for action. The gas was stinging their eyes; fear had sobered them up.

Thierry goaded Malard, and Malard lashed out with his club and missed him. Thierry ducked aside and sneered: 'You're still drunk, you old cunt.'

Bengston took his belt off, wrapped it round his right hand, and came towards them. The smell of the gas was beginning to fill the hallway. Now it was the vigilantes' turn to start coughing and rubbing their eyes. Majid was the first into the fray. He was met by a savage blow from a club, which he parried with his arm. The others piled in, and the vigilantes were driven back. Langlois was surprised by a kick in the belly that sent him sprawling. The kids were better fighters, and faster, and they began to get the upper hand. The alsatian barked, but didn't attack. Pat was like a tank when he got going. He demolished two of them all by himself. He grabbed Finet and pushed him against the plate-glass door so hard that it shattered. The battle raged on. Thierry had caught two powerful blows – one across the back and one across his shoulder – and was cornered against the lift door. Three of the old men were like dogs off the leash, kicking shit out of him even after he'd collapsed on the floor. Majid was defending himself as best he could. He managed to duck most of the blows that came his way. He grabbed a club off Finet – who was bent double in the hall doorway after the blow he'd received from Pat. Delphine tried to escape up the service stairs, and was pursued by Bonnaud. Miloud, his forehead all bloody, was putting up a brave fight, but they were too many for him and he had to flee under a hail of blows. Bengston was out for the count under the letterboxes, kayoed by a blow across the back of the neck. Majid and Pat were the only ones still holding out when the vigilantes decided to withdraw and call it a day. Pat followed them. Majid was on his knees, grimacing with pain, panting and holding his right arm. Miloud and Thierry were lying on the floor. Thierry was on his side, with his arms round his head, blocking the exit from the lift. He looked like he was sleeping. Pat came back, in a state of fury. He spat on the floor. Miloud was crying and complaining about the pain in his stomach. His left eye had an open cut over it, and the blood was running down his neck. Pat went over to see to Thierry, who was slowly regaining consciousness. Majid dragged Bengston up and shook him. The back of his neck was all bloody – a dirty blow.

'What about Fifine? And Farid?' Pat asked.

They went back to the cellar. Farid was sitting on the stairs with his back to the wall. He was coughing. He'd been there all through the fighting, still completely out of it. But there was no sign of Delphine. Pat suddenly realized what must have happened:

'Shit!'

They rushed to the service stairs and climbed

them four at a time. They found Fifine between the third and fourth floors. She was stretched out on the stairs, writhing in pain and crying bitterly. Pat raised her gently and picked her up in his arms.

That night, four cars went up in flames. The best fireworks display that Flower City had ever seen. People still talk about it, to this day.

That morning, Majid left the flat early. He had an appointment at the job centre. On the landing, the Levesque children, Fabienne and her kid brother, were waiting for the lift. They were off to school with their satchels on their backs. Little Fabienne saw Majid, but hung her head. She had a big black bruise round her right eye, that the kids at school would tease her about. Majid bent over and took her face in his hands.

'What happened,' he asked. She didn't answer and just stood there, shamefaced, with tears in her eyes.

Eric spoke up for his sister:

'It was dad.'

The lift arrived.

At the job centre, he was seen by an official who obviously couldn't be bothered with him. He opened Majid's file, and straightaway said:

'Nothing doing for you, friend!'

Majid swallowed. The man returned to his paper-work, and then pushed his glasses up onto his fore-head:

'You're fresh out of tech college, with no work

experience. It's going to be hard for us to find anything for you. Anyway, we have to give priority
to people who have rent to pay, families to raise,
and. . .'

'I see,' Majid cut in.

On the Pont Cardinet, Majid leans against the
balustrade and watches the trains come and go
into Gare Saint-Lazare. The afternoon is drawing
to an end. Every so often, he turns round, leans
against the railings, and watches the passers-by.

Pont Cardinet is a meeting place for homosexuals.
Majid waits.

Some of the guys look at him as they pass, but
they're not what he's looking for. They look lost
and broke. They walk to and fro across the bridge,
trawling, trying to look inconspicuous. There's half
a dozen of them, walking round, hands in their
pockets, newspapers under their arms.

Suddenly there's a new arrival. Very smart,
obviously well-off, aged about thirty, and wearing
an impeccable three-piece suit. A dynamic young
management type, not a hair out of place, clutching
his leather hand bag.

He passes close to Majid, brushes against him,
and continues on his way. Majid doesn't move;
he follows him with his eyes. When he's smiled
at, Majid smiles back, but stays where he is. The
man goes to the end of the bridge and turns again.
Majid looks his way and then walks off in the
opposite direction, towards the square. His prey
hesitates for a moment; then he starts to come
back. Majid walks slowly. The man follows him.

He obviously thinks he's struck lucky. He moves in a hurry.

By the time Majid reaches the square, the man is just a few yards behind him. The square is deserted. Majid walks along a grass verge next to a tall hedge. He walks without turning round, knowing he is being followed. Then, all of a sudden, Pat jumps out of the hedge and gives the man a powerful rabbit-chop across the back of the neck.

He falls to the ground and clutches at his neck as he curls up into a ball. His face is contorted with pain. Majid reaches into his jacket and relieves him of his wallet. Then they take off at speed.

They take a cab to the dance-hall. When he sees all the cars parked outside, Pat turns to Majid and says:

'Looks like it's going to be a good night!'

The dance-hall is near the lake at the edge of the Bois de Vincennes. Once inside, they head straight for the bar.

'Beer for me.'

'Two beers, please.'

Pat stands watching the dance-floor and drinking straight from the bottle. The disco lights are rotating, changing colours in time with the music. He devours the women with his eyes. There are women of every shape and kind. A dream.

Majid finishes his beer, puts the bottle back on the bar, and heads for the dance-floor. Pat follows him, letting out a blood-curdling 'Yippee!' He puts his bottle on a table next to the dance-floor and joins the dancers, leaping about like a lunatic. Stevie Wonder is too slow for his taste. Majid rises to the challenge.

They dance like this for a good quarter of an hour, eyes closed, alone with the music, just living for the present, living for themselves and feeling good. Then comes a series of slow numbers, so they return to the bar and order another couple of beers.

They check out the girls who are there in pairs. There aren't a lot. Choosing is the problem. They can't decide which pair to pull.

Finally they settle for two brunettes sitting at a table behind empty glasses. The girls look like they're bored. Pat says he fancies the one on the left, the one with the long hair. Majid says that's OK by him.

'You reckon they screw?'

'Let's hope so.'

'OK. Vamos.'

Pat gets to the girls first, and introduces himself. He asks the one with the long hair if she wants to dance. She smiles and gets up. Pat takes her hand and leads her off to the dance-floor. The other girl doesn't want to be upstaged by her friend, so she goes with Majid.

The two couples dance together on the circular dance-floor. When they catch each other's eye, Pat and Majid give each other a knowing wink. They dance another couple of slow numbers with the girls, just to be sure that they'd go all the way. 'Do you come here often?' Pat asks his brunette.

She smiles – the classic pick-up routine! By now, Majid is already kissing the other one on the neck and working his way up to her nose. Then they look into each other's eyes; she smiles, and they kiss on the mouth.

They take the girls and head back to the bar, where they down a few more beers. That's how the night passes – dancing, flirting, drinking and laughing. In the early hours of the morning, they come out of the dance-hall, arm in arm. The sudden cold makes them shiver. Pat cuddles up to his lady. Before she starts the car, she ask ironically:

'Where are we dropping you?'

Pat doesn't answer. He laughs out loud. Majid is stuck for an answer too.

'We'd better go home,' she says, 'because we've got work tomorrow.'

'We've got work too,' says Pat.

'We can't say goodbye just like that, though,' says Majid.

The girl starts the car and they set off at speed for a late-night drive through the Bois de Vincennes.

The brunette with the long hair turns to Pat, who is sitting on her right, and suggests:

'We could go back to our place, but you'll have to be quiet, OK?'

'OK.'

The girls have a studio in a brand-new apartment block near the Gare de Lyon.

Before getting down to business, Pat and Majid have a quick consultation in the toilet.

'You start with your one and I'll start with mine,' Pat whispers. 'And then we'll change over.'

'OK,' said Majid, as he washes his cock in the sink.

The lights go out, and they make love, each in their own corner. The silence is broken only by sighs and groans of pleasure.

The next morning at Gare Saint-Lazare, as they fought their way through the crowds of jostling commuters, Pat said:

'My one screwed better than yours.'

'Obviously,' said Majid. 'You had her first. By the time I got to her, she was knackered.' 'Be fair,' said Pat. 'My one was the best.'

'OK,' Majid conceded.

They boarded the train and went to sit at the end of the carriage. Majid wasn't entirely happy with Pat's comment, so he re-opened the debate:

'We'll ask Josephine which one of us screws best.'

'OK.'

They arrived home at about nine in the morning.

In the downstairs hallway, two women – one French and one Algerian – were arguing about something to do with their children, and calling each other every name under the sun. 'Your boy hit my daughter.'

'That's a lie!'

'He called her a dirty wog, too.'

'He was right.'

'Cunt!'

'And you.'

'Fuck off, you slag.'

'If you don't like it here, piss off back to your own country.'

The kids were crying and tugging at their mothers' skirts. One of the mothers ended up hitting her kids.

'Leave me alone. I'm going to fix that bitch.'

Majid and Pat waited for the lift. It was stuck somewhere. Pat gave the lift door a hefty kick, and they decided to take the service stairs. The women were still screaming at each other.

Rows of this sort were a daily event on the estate. Nobody even noticed any more. An inevitable result of the overcrowding.

When Majid got home, he found his mother waiting for him. 'What time do you call this to be coming home, eh?'

He went straight to his room, but she followed him.

'What about work? Have you found a job yet?'

He flopped onto the bed.

'Layabout. . . Lout. . .!'

She wailed and complained in Arabic. She called on Allah. She'd had enough. Majid shut his eyes and tried to sleep.

He was used to this kind of reception. And while his mother was insulting him, shouting at him, and complaining to Allah about him, Majid's mind was on sex. . .

Later in the afternoon, Pat was awakened by the sound of a siren. He swore when he looked out of his window and saw an ambulance and a police car. The ambulance men were gently lowering somebody onto a stretcher in the midst of a crowd of curious onlookers. He shaved quickly and went down.

He found Majid sitting on the hall steps, staring at the scene below. 'What's going on? The bastards woke me up.'

'It's Naima, Farid's sister,' Majid replied. 'You know, the one who never comes out because she's pregnant.' 'So?'

'She's had enough of being beaten up by her family. She's thrown herself out of the window.'

'For fuck's sake. . .! What about Farid?'

'He's in a terrible state. They've taken him too.'

The police car moved off. The crowd of onlookers stood back to make way for them. The sirens started again.

'Let's move.'

'Sure.'

They went down to Maggy's bar.

'I've got to see James,' said Majid.

'Why?'

'He's found a job. I wanted to ask if they're taking people on.'

'What's he do there?'

'Assembles stereos.'

They each took a turn on the pin-ball machine and got nowhere.

Pat asked, 'You serious?'

'Yeah. . . I've had enough of hanging out. . . and my mum crying every time I come home. . .'

'You make your bed. . .' Pat observed.

By the time James got back, it was late in the evening. He came straight from work. He said that the job wasn't difficult. He promised to introduce them to his foreman. They arranged to meet in front of the factory at seven o'clock the following morning.

'Look, lads, you won't mess things up for me, will you?' James said, as he went off. 'I don't want to get sacked.'

Malika is ironing shirts on the living-room table, and the children are quietly watching a film on the TV. Majid's there too, because it's cold outside, so he hasn't gone out again after bringing his dad back. The old man is sitting cross-legged on the carpet, leaning against the table-leg. He's watching the film, but there's no way of knowing if he understands what he's seeing. He stares at it intently, but there's no sign of recognition on his face. Majid sits alone, his head in his hands and his elbows resting on the table. He's waiting for midnight, when the girls of the Folies-Bergère are supposed to be on. Half undressed, they'll dance the can-can, as they do every New Year, and every New Year Majid dreams of screwing one of those chicks, with their legs like storks.

The stage settings, the choreography, and the music are all of no interest to him. He's only interested in the women. . . Look at them. . . those legs. . .! You'd need to live ten thousand years to get your fill of caressing them.

Malika is watching the dancers too. She puts her iron aside, sprawls in front of the TV, and remembers the days when she too used to sing and dance.

Majid remembers it well. He was a kid then, and he remembers his mother leading the dancing at family weddings in Algeria. The men would be on one side, and the women on the other, behind a mud wall. There would be about twenty women, in two rows, facing each other, and they would weave to and fro to the rhythm of the *bendir*, which Malika played with elegant pride. With her long black hair hidden behind the latest fashion in head-scarves, she would lead the singing. The songs they sang mocked their menfolk, as vulgar and pretentious.

Malika was beautiful – tall, young, and slender – and in those days she'd had only one child. Majid would come and tug at her dress, crying for her to pick him up. He'd have to wait until the dancing was over. Still, there was plenty of space to play, out in the north-west Algerian countryside, among the country folk who, in those days, knew nothing of city life and who were happy that way. The sun's rays were never absent – in fact its brilliance seemed to reflect its enjoyment of the dancing.

Stephane comes into the flat without knocking. Malika is surprised to see him there so early – and all alone too.

'Where's your mummy?' she asks, suddenly worried.

The child doesn't answer. He goes to talk with his friend Mehdi, who's on the bed in the living-room. Malika unplugs her iron and asks Amaria to put the clothes away for her. She goes out into the hallway and puts on her shoes and coat. She calls Majid and tells him to come with her. He is puzzled. 'Where are you going?' he asks.

'There must be something wrong,' she answers. 'The child's all alone, at this time of the day. I want to go and make sure Chousette's all right. Get a move on. . .!'

He scowls as he gets up. Amaria urges her brother to hurry, because she's worried too. So he gets dressed and follows his mother out to the lift.

The coarse, heavy, suburban snow has moulded itself to the pavement and is beginning to bury the parked cars. Two silhouettes cross the estate, making their way gingerly along the slippery pavements. Above their heads the concrete seems to turn pale as it merges with the grey sky. In the gutter the snow is melting fast, turning into a freezing slush which soaks through their shoes.

The building where Josette lives is surrounded by a lawn, but the grass is invisible beneath the snow, which is still falling. With his head sunk into his jacket, Majid has to hurry, because Malika is pressing ahead. He looks at his boots taking in water. His mother urges him to walk faster. 'Quick – go up to Chousette's flat.'

She raises her eyes to the balcony of Josette's flat, and urges him again, 'Hurry, hurry!'

Majid looks up and sees the reason for his mother's urgency. Josette is standing on the balcony, with her hands on the rail, looking straight in front of her. Malika steps over the little railings around the grass, looks up at the balcony, reaches up with both hands, and calls to Josette.

Majid goes up the service stairs four at a time, and arrives at her front door breathless. The door is shut.

Malika is still outside, screaming and waving
her arms at the balcony and trying to reason with
Josette.

But Josette is insensible to the cold and snow, and
deaf to her neighbour's pleas. Motionless, as if in a
trance, she stares at the distant horizon. The falling
snow half blinds Malika as she moves backwards
and forwards, begging Josette to open the door to
Majid. Some of the neighbours open their windows
to see who she's shouting at.

The coloured lights of the Christmas trees in
people's windows flash their festive message, but
Josette doesn't see them. All she sees is the black-
ness of a dark tunnel from which she never expects
to emerge. She's stuck there, abandoned, one of life's
failures. Her hands grip the balcony rail. Her tears
melt the snowflakes as they caress her cheeks. Her
mouth opens in a grimace of despair.

Malika is exhausted. She rushes to and fro, shouting herself hoarse. She doesn't know what more she
can say or do. One of the neighbours calls out:

'Best call the police. . .'

Majid comes down as fast as he went up, having
failed with the door. If only Jean-Marc had been
around, with his skeleton key. . . maybe he'd have
been able to open the door.

As Majid returns to his mum, he sees Josette putting one leg over the rail and beginning to move the
weight of her body over. Her arms are tired of hanging on – and her heart too. Majid rushes off to find
a phone, while Malika keeps talking, begging, and
then screaming as Josette finally puts her leg over
the rail.

'Chousette – don't do that! Chousette, think of Stephane! He'll cry when he's got no mummy.'

The boy's mother lies across the balcony rail, her face resting on the metal. She seems not to hear.

The phone box isn't working. Someone's stolen the handset. Majid runs to find another.

'I'll find you a job, Chousette, I'll find you a job in the school canteen – you can help with the meals. . .! Ya Chousette, ya Allah my God. . .'

Malika is on her knees in the snow. Helpless, the neighbours discuss what to do.

'Someone should call the police. . . the fire bri-gade. . .'

Nobody moves except the caretaker. He comes out of the building doing up his flies. He looks up, recog-nizes Josette, breathes on his hands to warm them, and announces to the assembled bystanders:

'She's the one who hasn't paid her rent for the past two months.'

Majid finds another phone box, but this one's completely wrecked. He has a sudden thought, and rushes back to his flat, taking care not to slip on the ice.

Malika is still praying to Allah, and calling to Josette not to throw herself off.

'It's a good place, Chousette. . . You'll work in the canteen. . . No problem. . . And you'll be all right there, Chousette. . . Please. . . Tomorrow, Chousette. . . I'll ask them for a job for you. . . It's a nice clean place. . . Good money. . .' As she begs and pleads, her coat turns white under the snow and her trembling hands reach up to the sky in supplication.

As Majid leaves the flat, he holds Stephane by the waist and presses him to his chest. He leaves as he'd arrived – running fast. The kid's got a toy in his hands – Babar the Elephant.

Josette is about to hurl herself into the void; her body is already half-sprawled over the side of the balcony. Majid puts Stephane down and points to his mother. The little one looks up, stares wide-eyed, moves forward to make himself heard, and shouts:

'Mummy, mummy, look what Mehdi's given me – Babar the Elephant.'

Josette moves her head. Maybe she's seen her son.

'Look, mummy,' Stephane repeats, waving his toy at her.

'It's your little boy. . .' Malika calls up to the balcony. 'Your little one.'

Josette lets herself slide slowly back from the rail, and slumps onto the balcony. Malika gets up, takes her head in her hands, and once again bursts into tears:

'Allah akbar!'

She allows her son to lead her off the snow-whitened lawn.

Majid turns to take one last look at Josette, as she lies on the balcony. All he can see is the snow falling on her.

The police arrive at the end of the street. Malika, Majid and Stephane step over the little barrier that runs round the building and make their way to the entrance-hall.

The caretaker is talking to the police and pointing up to the balcony where Josette is sprawled. Majid lights a cigarette and holds it with difficulty in his numbed fingers. Malika picks Stephane up and carries him up to his mother. She walks slowly, like a wanderer in the night, hugging the little blonde boy to her and crying as she goes.

Majid heads back to the tower-block. Through a half-open window on the ground floor, he hears the sound of a television. A voice is singing, 'A Happy New Year to One and All!'

The place was a proper little factory, installed on the first floor of an old building in Courbevoie. The boss was small, fat, and fortyish. He gave them each a pair of grey overalls and explained the job. It involved using a soldering iron in order to solder various wires and electrical components onto a printed circuit, all of which would eventually connect to the loudspeaker of a turntable. Then they were supposed to test it with a record. If no sound came out, they had to re-check the whole system from the start. They had ten boards to finish by mid-day, and the boss kept them at separate work-benches, to stop them talking.

James gave them an encouraging wink from the other end of the workshop. Pat was very relaxed about it all as he lit a cigarette and set to work. He found the whole business ridiculous and could barely restrain himself from laughing out loud. He switched on the soldering iron and picked it up.

Majid, on the other hand, got straight down to work, concentrating intensely, determined not to fail the test. The wages weren't brilliant, but it was still money.

The rest of the workforce – young kids for the

most part – were working flat out. On piece-work. No time to talk. Just keep on producing. When they lit a cigarette, they'd take one drag and then put it on the edge of the work-bench to burn away, because they couldn't take a second drag for fear of losing their rhythm.

It was obvious that Pat wasn't up to it. He couldn't care less, though. He watched Majid as he soldered away like an old hand.

The boss circulated among the lads to check their work and to supply them with fresh components. When he came to Pat, he leaned over to explain the job better. As soon as he turned his back again, Pat went back to ogling the girls in the office opposite. They smiled and gave him hasty little waves, because they were scared of being caught by the boss.

By ten o'clock, Majid was already finishing his fourth board. He looked over at Pat and saw that he'd barely finished his first.

Pat finally finished a board. He got up from his stool and plugged the turntable into a socket on the bench. He turned the 'on' switch and brought the arm across. Nothing happened.

'Doesn't seem to be working,' he said.

The boss unplugged the record-player, examined it, and was trying to explain something when Pat gave a sigh of boredom and said:

'Fuck it. . . I've had enough.'

'OK. . . fine. You can take your cards and leave.'

Pat looked at his watch.

'You still owe me for two hours, though.'

'Go down to the office. I'm coming.'

Majid stopped work as Pat passed him, heading in the direction of the office. Sacked!

Majid looked around him. The place was weird. Hundreds of cardboard boxes all over the place, shutting out the daylight, and all these kids, working, never looking up, never talking. . . And the song – always the same bloody song – every time they tested one of the record-players. He pulled out a cigarette and lit it.

In the office on the ground floor, the boss turned to a secretary seated at a typewriter and asked:

'Would you give this gentleman thirty francs, please.'

The secretary did as he said. Pat took the three ten-franc coins and left without a word. Outside in the street, the sun was just showing as he made his way towards Courbevoie station. He was about to turn right at the end of the street when he heard a whistle. He turned and saw Majid running after him. Pat shook his head.

'He thrown you out too?'

'If you like. . .' said Majid.

'You don't mean you walked out just because he sacked me?!'

'I didn't say that.'

'You're stupid you know. . .'

'*Me* stupid?! What about you. . .? Can't even solder a couple of wires onto a turntable.'

'So what? What's it to you, arsehole? I was just bored, all right?! The job was *boring*.'

'So what kind of job would Sir find interesting?'

'Shut up, for fuck's sake. . .'

'OK. Let's call it a day. . .'

Then they both fell silent, each lost in his own thoughts. They walked for a long time, through Courbevoie and on through Colombes. There was a hazy spring sun, and they felt like enjoying the snow. They were heading for Pont d'Argenteuil, with no idea of where they'd go after that. Pat called in at a bakery for a couple of croissants. An indoor tennis club caught their eye. All the courts were taken. Pat and Majid went in, drawn not so much by the game as by the women in their white mini-skirts.

'This lot must be rich,' Pat observed.

'Looks like only the rich play tennis. Seems like they don't eat either – it's lunchtime and they're still coming in. Look.'

'Makes you fat if you eat. They have to stay skinny so as to pull the chicks.'

That'll be good news in the Sudan!'

'Somebody should write and tell them. Might cheer them up while they're starving.'

'They'd eat the letter. . . out of sheer rage.'

'Look at the arse on that one, the one who's just missed her smash.'

'I wouldn't mind going a set with her. . .'

'They can't even bloody play!'

'It's just for show.'

Two other couples emerged from the changing rooms, rackets in hand and dressed in whites. Pat watched them and thought for a moment.

'What say we do the changing rooms?'

'Trouble is, these sporty types run fast. . . They don't like parting with their money. . .'

'You'll see. . . It's a piece of piss. . . Must be plenty of cash in there. . . Come on, let's go.'

Cautiously they skirted the hedges surrounding the courts. They went round the back of the building and found a little alleyway between the hedge and the changing rooms. Each changing room had its own window, which meant they could check which room had the most clothes in it. They picked their room, but this wasn't their lucky day; the window was locked. So Pat picked up a stone the size of his fist and broke the glass. Then they waited for a moment to see if anyone had heard. Pat reached inside and opened the window. 'Up you go,' he said.

Majid climbed up on the rail, jumped down into the changing room, and carefully jammed a chair under the door-handle to stop anyone coming in. Then Pat joined him, and they searched every pocket in the place. Having taken all the banknotes and big coins, they carefully put back the empty wallets and purses. Before they went out of the main gate, Pat signalled to Majid to stop. The club caretaker was moving across the central roadway pushing a broom. They waited until he'd gone into the hut. Then they sauntered out, casually. Once they were outside, Pat turned round to check that nobody was following them. Then they started running for the station. They fell about laughing, and only stopped when they reached the long railway bridge between the Gare du Stade and the Gare de Colombes.

Pat patted his pockets and spluttered, 'What a haul!'

Panting for breath, they still had the strength

to laugh. 'Look out, Paris! Here come the out-of-townies!' said Majid.

The obvious place to blow the money was to go into town, so they headed off to their favourite stamping-grounds. They stopped for a merguez and chips, and beer, and more beer. Once they'd eaten their fill, they went to rue Saint-Denis to get an eyeful of the prostitutes. In the doorway of a hotel stood two big, heavily made-up girls, wearing nothing but a pair of knickers under their open-fronted fur coats. They lingered there, their mouths watering. A third girl was sitting on the hotel steps, her legs apart. Pat nudged Majid:

'Jesus, look at her, she's got no knickers on.'

Majid leaned across to see.

'I can't see a thing!'

'Tasty!'

'Look at those tits!'

'Look at that one,' said Pat. 'The black one on the pavement, over there.'

'A pro and a half!'

'Look at those lips,' Pat enthused. 'Imagine them sucking you off!'

'My dick fancies taking a little dip!'

'Well go ahead, then.'

'I can't decide which one,' Majid admitted.

'What about that one over there! Built to last, that one!'

They stopped in front of a bar. Pat scanned the horizon.

'. . .Or that one, the one on her own, with the green hat.'

Majid saw her, standing on her own about fifty yards off, in the doorway of a small hotel. She was wearing tight-fitting black shorts, a denim jacket, and high-heel shoes.

'Looks not bad,' said Pat.

'Yeah. . . There's not too many punters about, either,' said Majid, to give himself a bit of courage.

'Go on, then. I'll wait for you back here.'

Majid crossed the road, and turned to see if anyone was looking. It was the middle of the afternoon, so there weren't as many punters as in the evening. Just as well, because at a time like this, you want to be on your own and out of sight.

He went up to the prostitute, self-consciously, but driven by lust. She didn't see him coming up. All you could see of her was her legs and her hand as she raised her cigarette to her lips. Majid made a sudden approach, and with one step he was inside the building and standing next to her. All of a sudden, his brain signalled red alert. He scratched his head as his eyes opened wide in amazement. Talk about a surprise!

It was Chantal, Pat's sister. She gaped at him, went white as a sheet, and didn't say a word. He was thoroughly embarrassed too; he was so surprised that he could only say: 'I'm sorry.'

He stepped back a bit and added:

'Why do I always end up in these situations?'

Chantal stubbed her cigarette out on the floor and made a gesture that said, 'Don't go.' She finally managed to open her mouth, but nothing came out. She shook her head, completely at a loss.

'You won't say anything, will you. . .? Not to anyone!' she begged. He stepped back again:

'No, I won't. . . Don't worry. . . I promise. . .'

She came towards him, still pleading:

'You haven't seen me, Majid, all right?'

He pushed her back into the hallway.

'Don't go out. Your brother's waiting for me outside.' Chantal was suddenly scared again. She blushed deeply and covered her face with her hands.

'Has he seen me?'

'No, no,' Majid reassured her. 'And I won't say a word.'

He was about to leave when she called him back and began rummaging in her handbag. 'No, no,' he interrupted her. 'I don't want anything.'

'Yes.'

He was already off down the street. What a fuck-up! All of a sudden, his dick no longer fancied taking a little dip. Without looking back he returned to the bar, where Pat was waiting for him.

Pat was at the pinball machine. He was so surprised to see Majid back so soon that he lost his ball down the hole.

'Tell you what, we're going to call you Colt .45, you're so quick on the draw. Ha, ha! Nice one, you old lecher!'

Majid ordered a beer so as not to have to answer straight away.

'I didn't do it,' he said.

'Eh? Why not?'

'I lost my nerve.'

'Lost your nerve, ha, ha! You've got no balls!'

Majid was not amused. He took a mouthful of beer, to calm himself.

Later in the afternoon they headed off to score some dope. For a while now the local dealers had been operating out of an underground car park in Belleville. Their regular man arrived on the dot of six o'clock – short and stocky, dressed all in leather, with a beard and dark glasses. They bought two blocks of Lebanese.

As usual, Pat was careful to check the quality of the stuff.

The dealer never spoke, except when the price of a gramme had gone up. Then he'd announce the new price. Occasionally he'd give them an alternative rendezvous.

They took their dope and left.

Night was already falling by the time they got back to the estate.

'Shall we go to Maggy's?' Pat asked.

'No. I'm going to get my dad.'

Pat went with him. Majid stopped to piss against a wall. With all the beers he'd sunk that afternoon, he was having to piss every half hour. Pat too. They were both standing there, faces to the wall, when a BMW came speeding round the corner. The car drove past them, then stopped thirty yards down the road. Pat closed his flies. The car reversed back to them. They heard the sound of Bengston's shrill laugh. Anita was sitting in the back. She called to them to get in.

Pat was in the mood for taking the piss:

'We can't. He's got to go looking for daddy.'

General laughter from inside the car.

Majid, who was still half-drunk, answered: 'What the hell. . . I deserve it!'

Jean-Marc, who was driving, hooted the horn. Thierry stuck his little weasel face out of the window:

'Come on, get in. Let's move.'

'OK. What the fuck,' said Majid.

And that was how he ended up in that BMW. Needless to say, Pat also fancied a ride. The car sped off with its tyres screeching. They took the Nanterre motorway, driving flat-out. Pat brought out his block of Lebanese and asked Anita to roll a joint. When he saw the dope, Bengston let out a joyful 'Yippee'. Thierry clapped his hands.

'Where did you get that?' asked Jean-Marc.

'Did I ask where you got this motor. . .?'

'It's his dad's,' Bengston chimed in. 'He said we could take it for a spin.'

Everyone fell about laughing. Then Thierry said:

'I've got an idea. . .'

'You and your bright ideas. . . Best keep them to yourself,' said Anita. 'Last time, we all wound up in the cop-shop.'

Thierry explained that this time it was a good one.

'Go ahead – let's hear it,' said Bengston.

'Why don't we go to the seaside?'

The others looked at each other. Then Jean-Marc said:

'Why not?!'

Anita objected that she hadn't brought her swimming costume.

'Skinny-dipping!' shouted Pat. 'Ha, ha! Really, though. . .'

Jean-Marc turned to Majid:

'What d'you say. . .? We go to Deauville?'

'Cut the cackle and step on the gas,' said Majid.

'No need to get upset. I was just saying. . . Seeing that they want to go to the seaside, and since you'd rather go looking for your dad, I just wondered. . .'

Another round of laughter. Then Pat slapped
Jean-Marc on the shoulder:

'Put your foot down!'

Bengston was asking for the joint, so Anita lit it
and handed it to him. Majid shut his eyes and let
sleep overtake him. On the motorway, Jean-Marc
pushed the motor flat-out, overtaking everything in
sight. He was enjoying himself:

'Eat dirt, you wankers!'

'And tomorrow morning we'll be chatting up all
the middle-class women in Deauville,' said Pat.
'Ha, ha!'

'You mean the old ladies. . .' Bengston asked.

'Yeah – the old ladies with pots of money.'

'We'll go halves on them.'

'Not you, though.'

'Why not, pray?'

Because middle-class ladies don't like nig-nogs,
that's why,' Pat proclaimed.

'Why not?' asked Bengston, sitting up.

Pat paused for a moment before taking a draw on
the joint:

'Well, they might like nig-nogs to screw with, but
they won't go out with them.'

'How do you know?' said Thierry.

'This summer,' said Pat, 'me and Majid are going
to the south coast. We'll have a gas there!'

He blew out the smoke from the joint and
explained what he had in mind. 'It's easy. You go
plant yourself on one of those terrace cafés where
they go to drink their tea. You find one who doesn't
look too much like an old granny. She notices you.
Zap! You give her a sweet little smile, and she wets

her knickers. Her husband's sitting next to her. He sees you, but doesn't say a word. He should worry! He's a poof. They're all poofs, middle-class men. . . they all prefer a good wank, and their wives get pissed off with it. You stay on the terrace. You give her the eye again. She smiles back. What does she do then? She takes her bag and goes off to the toilet. While she's in there, she writes her phone number on a piece of paper. Then she comes back. She turns to her husband and says, "Shall we go?" Off they go, and she lets him pass so's she can follow behind. As she passes your table, she slips you the piece of paper with her number. Then all you have to do is phone her one evening. She invites you to her villa up on the hill, with big iron railings and trees all around. You push the button on the entry-phone at the gate, and you hear a sexy voice saying, "I'm coming, honey." You've got a hard-on already. You cross the garden and go up the front stairs. She opens the door. The slag's wearing a white see-through bathrobe. She takes your hand and leads you to an armchair. You act all innocent, and you get an eyeful of her arse, which is white, because she always keeps her bikini bottom on when she's sunbathing. You sit down. She takes your jacket. Then she says, "What would you like? Whisky? Champagne?" She pours you a glass. She raises her glass and gives you a sexy look: "Your health." She puts the glass down and hands you a box of cigars. You take one and she lights it for you. You take a drag and sink back into the armchair. You shut your eyes. Then you feel her fingers opening your flies. You're on your way, pal!

'You give her a good old proletarian ding-dong.

You shag her till she drops. Give her something to remember you by. Then, when it's over, she stuffs a wad of banknotes into your pocket. You go back to see her often, and she introduces you to her daughter, her mother and her sister, and you screw them too. No mercy! And all the while, her husband's poncing around on his yacht!'

Jean-Marc interrupted: 'Very interesting story. Look, it's sent Majid to sleep.

'Let him sleep. I've told him it before.'

'You ever screwed a rich woman?' asked Thierry.

'No, but it'll come. I'm telling you. . . Majid and me, we're spending the summer down on the coast.'

'How am I ever going to end up rich,' sighed Anita, 'if rich men are all queers?'

'You've got no chance,' said Pat. 'They can't run after chicks and count their money at the same time. Can't be done!'

It was dead of night when they arrived at the seaside. A gentle breeze was blowing along the beach. They left the car on the road, and ran, laughing, to the water's edge. Majid lagged behind for a bit, and then hurried and caught up with them. He wasn't feeling up to it. They started pushing each other into the sea. 'We going in for a swim?' suggested Pat.

'Too cold,' Thierry replied.

'I'm going back to the car. I'm cold,' said Anita.

Jean-Marc followed her.

Pat took a deep breath and threw out his chest. He smiled at Majid and said:

'That's sobered you up, eh?'

Majid stared at the dark horizon, with his hands in his pockets and his hair blowing in the wind. He was feeling restless, like he was bored. They all returned to the car.

'It's a lot nicer in the warm,' Anita purred.

'You don't say!' said Bengston.

When Majid got back into the car, Pat could see he was out of sorts.

'What's up?' he asked.

'It's OK. . . Nothing,' said Majid, with an effort.

'Oh God, he's in one of his moods. . .'

The car moved off up the stony road, its headlights cutting through the darkness of the sleeping countryside. Tiredness slowly got the better of them, all except for Pat and Jean-Marc, which was just as well, because Jean-Marc was driving. Anita yawned.

'Everyone asleep in here?' Pat bawled.

He looked round the car and then prodded Thierry. 'I'm awake,' said Thierry. 'And to prove it, look, there's a car ahead. Those lights, just round the bend. Watch out, Jean-Marc.'

The BMW was cruising gently. Visibility was poor. Majid was dozing off, dead to the world. He just wanted to sleep.

'Shit — it's the cops!'

Jean-Marc saw it first. The others sat up. There, in front of them, was the unmistakable blue flashing light of a patrol car. 'Keep going, don't stop,' said Pat. 'Act normal. If they block the road, it's everyone for themselves.'

He woke Majid and pointed to what lay ahead. Majid looked up, saw the patrol car suddenly

stop dead in the middle of the road, and saw
a cop get out. Jean-Marc jammed on the brakes
and yelled:

'Make a run for it!'

They dived out of the car and fled across the fields.
Before he went Pat yelled at Majid: 'Get a fucking
move on!'

Majid looked like he didn't want to leave his seat.
He just stared straight in front of him, his eyes
half-closed, fed up and tired. Pat ran off behind
the others. One of the cops gave chase, but then
gave up and came back all out of breath. The sergeant leaned into the BMW. He took a long look
at Majid and told him to come out. Majid obeyed
without a word. His head bowed, he went and sat
in the patrol car.

'Now we've got this one, we'll soon get the rest,'
said the sergeant, looking over to where Pat and the
others had disappeared.

The patrol car moved off, followed by the BMW,
which was being driven by one of the cops. The sergeant turned to look at Majid; he was now wearing
handcuffs, and they'd fixed the handcuffs to a bar on
the back seat.

'So where do you and your pals come from?'

Majid didn't reply. His head lolled back against
the head-rest and he closed his eyes.

The sergeant let him be. The patrol car cruised
on until it came to a well-lit crossroads out in the
middle of the countryside.

At the crossroads, lo and behold, there was
Pat, sitting on a milestone. He got up as the
flashing blue lamp swept him with its light. He

took a drag on his cigarette. He signalled to the patrol car to stop, as if he was flagging down a bus.

'Who's he?' asked the sergeant.

Pat stubbed out his cigarette on the gravel and got into the car.

'I was with him,' he said, pointing to Majid.

He sat down, facing his friend. Majid was asleep. Pat looked at him. The patrol car cruised off into the night.